Perihelion Summer

ALSO BY GREG EGAN

Diaspora
Dichronauts
Distress
Incandescence
Permutation City
Quarantine
Schild's Ladder
Teranesia
Zendegi

THE ORTHOGONAL SERIES
The Clockwork Rocket
The Eternal Flame
The Arrows of Time

SHORT STORY COLLECTIONS
Oceanic
Luminous
Axiomatic

PERIHELION SUMMER

GREG EGAN

A TOM DOHERTY ASSOCIATES BOOK

NEW YORK

PERIHELION SUMMER

Copyright © 2019 by Greg Egan

Cover art and design by Drive Communications

Edited by Jonathan Strahan

A Tor.com Book
Published by Tom Doherty Associates
175 Fifth Avenue
New York, NY 10010

www.tor.com

Tor® is a registered trademark of
Macmillan Publishing Group, LLC.

ISBN 978-1-250-31377-5 (ebook)
ISBN 978-1-250-31378-2 (trade paperback)

First Edition: April 2019

PART ONE

1

Matt's parents threw a party for New Year's Eve, filling the house and garden with people and food, music and liquor. His mother had sent invitations to the rest of the crew, but Matt knew that on their last night before departing they'd choose to be with their own families instead, so he was left with the company of relatives and acquaintances who all believed that he'd lost his mind.

It was a sweltering night, and even in the yard the floodlights obliterated any trace of the stars and left him claustrophobic. Most people were polite to his face, though when he saw them watching out of the corner of his eye, some looked dismayed, as if he'd joined an apocalyptic death cult and was on his way to Heaven's Gate, while others were smirking with what he supposed was condescending amusement at the absurdity of his actions.

As the night wore on, some guests became less inhibited. "How many years did you work on Greater Sunrise?" Matt's cousin Leo demanded, cornering him beside the barbecue.

"Five," Matt replied.

"Fly-in, fly-out?"

"Yes. Six weeks on, two weeks off."

"For what? Two hundred grand a year?"

"That's what I was getting at the end," Matt conceded. "Before tax."

"Two hundred grand, for working on the rigs! Straight out of university!"

"No," Matt corrected him. "There was a two-year traineeship first. On about one-fifth the salary."

Leo was undeterred. "You could have bought a house! Or at least put down a deposit!"

"Probably."

"But now you're off for a cruise in the *SS Sunk Costs*, just to make us all believe it was worth it."

Matt wasn't sure why his cousin was quite so affronted by the way he'd spent his money, unless he subscribed to some kind of Tinker Bell effect whereby the mere act of investing in real estate served as a show of faith that would help render everyone's bricks and mortar invulnerable.

He said, "We'll be testing out a form of aquaculture that could help a lot of people. I think that's worth all the time and money we've put into it, regardless."

"Regardless?" Leo snickered. "So when you're back here in six months, and the sky hasn't fallen, you can pretend you've saved face because it was all about world hunger?"

Matt said, "Nothing would make me happier than being able to come back."

"You're drunk, Leo. Go and lie down." Matt turned; his sister Selena was standing beside him.

Leo opened his mouth to protest, but Selena gazed back at him sternly and he walked away without another word.

"How do you do that?" Matt marveled.

"Unwavering self-belief," she replied. "It only lasts twenty seconds at a time, but that's long enough for most purposes."

Matt was tongue-tied for a moment. Then he said, "The invitation still stands. Bring Mum and Dad if you can talk them into it—and I know you could, if you used your lawyer's superpowers."

Selena smiled. "You really think we're doomed here?" She spoke without a trace of sarcasm, but also without a trace of fear.

Matt framed his reply carefully, struggling to find the right balance between overselling the risk and talking it down. "On the *Mandjet,* we'll be self-sufficient in food, and pretty much immune to sea-level changes. So why not take advantage of that, if you have a choice?"

Selena said, "I live on high ground. I have solar panels,

a rainwater tank, and enough food in the freezer to last a year."

"I think you're exaggerating the size of your freezer."

"There's a lot of dry pasta in the pantry as well."

Matt tried pushing harder. "If the ocean rises fifty meters in a day, and the high-tide mark is twenty kilometers inland, will you still be glad you stayed put?"

Selena shook her head. "No. But most of the experts think the chances are good that Taraxippus won't come close enough to make any difference at all."

"That's true." Matt laughed, sick to his stomach at the realization that he was almost certainly powerless to sway her. He was already so accustomed to the particular kind of austerity he was about to face that another few months surrounded by ocean, with limited privacy, rudimentary hygiene and multiple sources of unpleasant odors seemed like a perfectly fair price to pay against odds of five-hundred-to-one that it would turn out to be a life-or-death decision. But if he'd spent the last few years in oak-paneled offices and a comfortable suburban home, the idea of being cooped up on a floating fish farm just to better his prospects in an unlikely apocalypse would probably have struck him as disproportionate, if not actually deranged.

He said, "The error bars might shrink over the next few weeks. If you change your mind, we won't be too far off the coast. Say the word, and I'll find a way for you to join us."

"Okay." Selena managed to sound entirely sincere, without conceding the slightest possibility of any of these things happening.

She reached out and embraced him. "Just keep yourself safe," she said. "Even in the best of times, nothing's unsinkable."

2

Matt met Arun at the marina and they set off for the *Mandjet* in the runabout. The swell was about three meters, but there was almost no wind, and once they were out on the open water the waves were glassy, rolling in every ten or twelve seconds, leaving the boat rising and falling like a fairground ride stuck in a time loop.

"Are you as hungover as you look?" Arun asked, shouting over the noise of the outboard. He had yet to remove his own sunglasses, but then, it was a bright morning.

Matt said, "I didn't drink much. But I didn't get much sleep. How was your send-off?"

"My mother wouldn't stop crying."

"She thinks she won't see you again?"

"No, she thinks I've made myself a laughingstock and I'll never work again."

"Okay." Matt didn't know what more they could have done to distance themselves from the crackpots, who believed that the encounter was a fait accompli predicted by the Mayans or the Babylonians, and orchestrated in fine detail by malevolent aliens. His team had never disputed the astronomers' claims about the distribution of possible trajectories for the black hole; why would they, when every observation was on the public record, and anyone with a computer and a grasp of undergraduate physics could verify the whole analysis for themselves? In any case, the *Mandjet* was a perfectly respectable venture that was worth pursuing for a dozen different reasons—and when they'd shared the design on the internet, they hadn't included one word about Taraxippus. "We can't win," he decided.

Arun grinned, his dark lenses glinting. "Not unless it goes badly on land."

Matt's skin crawled. "Don't say that."

"So now you're getting superstitious about what we *say*?"

"No. But if we joke about it, and it happens, won't you feel bad?"

"Not for joking about it," Arun insisted. "I'll feel bad for not feeding my family sleeping pills and dragging them out here against their will."

Matt glanced at the brown cloth sack on the floor of the boat, but it wasn't really large enough even for Arun's youngest sister.

He checked the GPS, then turned the motor a little to correct their course. After a few minutes, each time the waves lifted the runabout he could see the glint of sunlight off the *Mandjet*'s solar panels, and before long the bright flashes were joined by glimpses of orange fiberglass. The broad ring of linked pontoons was draped over the undulating surface of the water like a Dali clock; one unkind online commenter had described the vessel as "flotsam that hadn't yet had time to disperse." But the more the individual segments seesawed up and down beside their neighbors, the more power they generated in the links. "Let's see you do that with a pile of floating steamer trunks," Arun had replied.

As they drew up beside the docking pen, Matt saw the second runabout in place, which meant Yuki and Jožka were already on board. He maneuvered the boat into the pen and then the two of them each took a line and jumped onto the dock. The runabout pulled away, but Arun already had his line snagged on a cleat, and between them it only took a couple of minutes to get the thing secured. Matt walked around and closed the gate of the pen, then returned to find Arun shouldering his mysterious sack.

Matt grabbed his own, much smaller backpack. "Should I even ask what's in that?"

Arun shook the sack gently; Matt heard tins and glass clanking. "One of my aunts insisted on offering her idea of suitable provisions, and I didn't have the heart to refuse."

"No harm in that. There's more to life than cobia."

Arun grunted in reluctant assent. "A clean break might have been easier, though. There I was, reconciled to an indefinite abstinence from mango chutney, and now I have to start wondering all over again what it will feel like when the supply runs out."

They climbed the ladder to the deck. Matt glanced down into the enclosed circle of water—though short of a mass die-off or a sudden algal bloom, nothing on the surface was likely to reveal any clues about the health of the passengers below. "No shark fins," he noted.

Arun took off his sunglasses and regarded him with horror. "So we can joke about *that*?"

"Sure, if by 'we' you mean anyone who volunteers to help me fix holes in the net."

They reached one of the links just as the footbridge spanning the gap above the pivot was starting to lengthen. While the extra meter or so of supporting rods and safety rails emerged from the housings for the pumps they were driving, the deck of the bridge simply concertinaed out, its tiny flexing parallelograms tickling the soles of Matt's feet.

As they rounded the corner, Matt saw a pale young man leaning over the rail, vomiting a yolk-yellow stream into the Indian Ocean.

"Do you know who that is?" he asked Arun.

"No idea."

"It's not Jožka's brother?"

"I don't think so."

Yuki emerged from her cabin and put an arm tenderly across the man's shoulders. She spotted her two friends approaching and frowned, as if they were intruding on a private moment, before turning back to the ailing man.

Matt stopped walking. "Did you know she had a new boyfriend?"

"No. I'm not in the loop; you're the one who told me when she broke up with what's-his-name."

Matt looked away from the couple, trying to suppress his sense of disquiet. They were all entitled to bring as many companions as the *Mandjet* could feed and house; that was the whole point of the venture. And if he'd managed to persuade Selena to join him, she'd certainly be throwing up about now. But even if his friends only knew his sister slightly, they knew he could vouch for her. How long had Yuki known this man?

The man wiped his mouth with the back of his hand, and the two of them reentered the cabin.

Matt looked to Arun for guidance. "So do we go and introduce ourselves, or wait until he stops barfing?"

Arun said, "I think it would be rude to wait that long."

When they reached the entrance, Matt saw that Jožka was also in the cabin. She was holding a fixed, polite smile, but when she glanced at Matt it slipped a little.

Yuki said, "Aaron, this is Matt and Arun."

Arun stepped forward and shook Aaron's hand. "It won't be confusing at all," he assured him. Aaron stared back at his homophonic twin with slitted eyes, too nauseous even to smile.

Matt said, "It'll get better, I promise."

"You mean the waves will die down?" Aaron asked hopefully.

"Only the peristaltic ones."

Yuki said, "Can we have some space?"

"Sure," Matt replied. The three of them left the cabin and made their way around the ring toward the control room.

"So have you met this guy before?" Arun asked Jožka.

"No. The first I heard of him was this morning, when he showed up at the marina with Yuki."

"Any idea what he does?"

"He blogs about TV shows."

"You mean he's on the dole?"

"No, I think he gets a grant from the One Blog Per Blowhard Foundation."

"Sounds like you two really hit it off before the vomiting started."

Jožka's expression softened a little, but she was still bemused. "After all the people we pleaded to join us . . . I think Yuki's only known him for a couple of weeks. It's hard to imagine him sticking it out for the entire window."

Matt didn't want to rush to judgment—and in a sense it didn't matter now. "Well he's here, so he's made a commitment."

Arun guffawed. "To what, though?"

"To the same thing as all of us," Matt insisted. "I don't care if he's done a comprehensive risk analysis, or if he's just besotted, as long as he completes the safety induction and helps out with the maggots."

Arun seemed to find that even funnier. "You honestly think he *knows* about the maggots?"

Matt smiled, trying to imagine Yuki raising the subject on the dance floor of her favorite nightclub. "Anyway, we've got to be fair to both of them. If we start forming in-groups and out-groups already..." He didn't finish the sentence; talking about sharing the vessel with a hundred starving, bedraggled strangers felt like a surreal, pretentious interjection into a conversation about one crew member's seasick slacker boyfriend.

When they reached the control room, Matt and Jožka entered, while Arun went to stow his aunt's gifts in the mess. Matt took off his backpack and sat down at the console. The batteries and the compressed-air stores were fully charged; if they'd been closer to shore, they could have been selling their excess power. The freshwater tanks were near capacity. The temperature and chemical profile for the cobias' giant pond looked fine, and Yuki's flies seemed content in their fly heaven, dining for the moment mostly on fish carcasses and rotting seaweed. None of the sensors in the garden were flagging insect attacks, or wilting leaves.

Jožka said, "After the window passes, we should sell this to some seasteader billionaire."

"Don't you think they'll have all built their own already?"

"Ours is nicer," she insisted.

Matt laughed. "Ours is *cheaper*. If you're used to the Hilton, swaying floors are probably a deal breaker."

The satellite link was displaying a satisfying row of green lights, but Matt restrained himself from wasting kilobytes checking the web for new observations. The system he'd set up on the old computer in his parents' home would email him if there was anything worth knowing—with better criteria for which sources were reliable than poor, gullible Google, whose algorithms seized upon, and amplified, every random act of Taraxippus-trolling, and every innocent-but-baseless, exponentially inflating rumor.

"I have absolutely nothing to do," he declared, leaning back in the chair and sighing contentedly.

Jožka smiled.

"What?"

She said, "Check the roster. The maggots are calling your name."

3

Matt was woken by a gentle but insistent buzz—the tone he'd chosen for system issues with no immediate safety implications. He opened his eyes and checked his watch: it was just after three A.M. He was tempted to go back to sleep; in two hours he'd have daylight and a fully functioning brain, both of which were likely to make any problem easier to address.

But as soon as the buzzing stopped, he knew that if he stayed in bed he'd just lie awake wondering about the cause. He rolled off his bunk and fished his phone out of its pocket on the wall.

He squinted at the text on the over-bright screen. The satellite provider had sent him a message saying that he'd used 95 percent of his account's quota, and if he hit the limit the connection would be unavailable for anything but calls to emergency services. Another message had arrived about half an hour earlier, informing him that he'd crossed the 75 percent mark. He'd never thought to trigger an alarm at that point; it usually meant that they had days of normal usage remaining.

He pulled on a T-shirt and left the cabin. The navigation lights dulled the sky around the horizon, but when he glanced up at the zenith it was like the view from a starship.

He made his way around the ring, walking beside the fluorescent safety strips. When he reached the control room, he sat down at the console and tried to recall where the network's usage would be logged in detail. He didn't want to pull the plug on the satellite link immediately, only to find that when he reconnected it, the meter had kept ticking away, thanks to some error in the company's servers or some hacker spoofing his account.

Matt found the log. The satellite provider hadn't made an error. But before he could decide what to do, the final message came through: the quota was used up.

He walked around to Yuki and Aaron's cabin, and knocked on the door, as gently as he could bring himself to do. It was Aaron who opened it, and he spoke before Matt could. "Is your WiFi down too?" he whispered. He was holding two earbuds in one hand, as if he'd taken them out on his way to the door.

Matt said, "Did Yuki not tell you?"

"Tell me what?"

"About the quota."

"No."

Matt looked past him into the cabin; it was in darkness, except for a glowing iPad lying on one of the bunks, a frozen image filling the screen. "Okay. Well, it's a lot less than you're probably used to. And you just exhausted it."

"Oh." Aaron managed an embarrassed smile. "Sorry. It was the season finale of *Lilliput . . .*" He stopped, perhaps intuiting that, at sea, there was no extenuating clause that involved season finales. "I'll pay for whatever it cost you."

Matt said, "Forget about the money. You need to start thinking about where the fuck you are."

"No one told me!" Aaron protested.

"Do you see any towers on the horizon? Could you really not have guessed that that would make a difference? Or even wondered, and asked?"

"Yuki was asleep."

"You couldn't wait until tomorrow?"

Aaron had no reply. Matt turned and walked away.

Back in his cabin, he tried to calm himself, willing the self-righteous adrenaline out of his veins. It would be a tiny thing to fix: at first light, he'd take one of the runabouts, and once he was in range of a tower he'd be able to top up the contract in a matter of minutes. Aaron had been on board less than a day; he had no experience with the environment, and he wasn't a mind reader. Making a big thing out of one small error of judgment would be unfair.

Matt lay down on his bunk and closed his eyes, but

sleep remained elusive. He'd thought he'd been prepared for any number of last-minute passengers—and there was no doubt that the *Mandjet* could meet the material needs of at least two dozen in comfort, and four times as many at a stretch. On the rigs, he'd often slept in rooms with eight people, of four or five nationalities, and they'd usually managed to keep their disputes from escalating. He hadn't seen so much as a fistfight in all of his time offshore.

But then, his fellow workers had been trained and vetted, and they'd all had far too much to lose to let any petty irritations get under their skin. And every six weeks, they could leave the sardine cans on stilts and go let off steam however they liked.

He wasn't *prepared*. There was no rehearsing any of this. All he could do was keep hoping that the *Mandjet*'s extra cabins would prove superfluous, and a few hours without the internet would mark the height of their tribulations.

4

Matt finished filling the bucket with maggots, then skimmed one more shovelful of the squirming white mass from the top of the compost and delivered it into the hopper leading to the maturation chamber. Then he made his way carefully across the swaying deck and tossed the contents of the bucket into the encircled water.

As always, the meal sank without a trace. It would have been nice if the recipients could bother staging some kind of feeding frenzy, setting the water roiling in a show of appreciation just to convince him that he wasn't wasting his time. But Matt had never seen a single uneaten larva among the fish feces and other crud that the recycling system pumped up from the depths of the pond.

He stood for a moment savoring the breeze, then noticed a faint tickling sensation; he glanced down to find a couple of stragglers clinging to his chest, and flicked them off over the rail. As he'd shoveled the maggots, their stench seemed to have permeated his skin, more from proximity than actual contact, until even his own sweat stank of fish oil. There was no stage in any insect's life cycle when it was entitled to smell more piscine than an actual fish—and while the flies' CRISPR'd genes and algal supplements added all the right oils needed to provide the cobia with a balanced diet, every human Matt had ever met found that the incongruous odor made the wriggling larvae even more disgusting than their unaltered cousins.

As he turned away from the rail, he saw Yuki approaching. She stopped suddenly, and Matt wondered why, then he realized that he was scowling.

"What's up?" he asked cheerfully.

"There's been another lensing," she said. She did not sound happy, but she offered no more details.

Matt nodded. "I'll be there in a minute."

He went to the saltwater shower by the fly hut and stood under the flow, until the odor of maggots and compost was either gone, or overpowered by the water's notes of brine and algae. He shook himself half-dry, and then the walk back to his cabin in the morning sun baked most of the remaining droplets from his skin, so he barely needed to use a towel.

When he arrived in the control room Jožka was seated at the console, with the others gathered around her.

"So what's the news?" he asked.

Jožka said, "The ring's nowhere near big enough. It's very confusing."

"You mean the arcs are too small?" Matt nudged Arun; he was a head taller than Matt, and he let him squeeze closer to the console to grant them both an unimpeded view. The image, taken at Cerro Armazones, showed the starlight that had passed close to the black hole spread into two arcs that were each barely more than quarter-circles. The hole needed to cross right in front of the star to yield the full circle of an Einstein ring; if it was off-target only parts of the circle appeared. But the astronomers knew how to extract results when the alignment was far less perfect than this; they didn't need an unbroken ring.

"I mean the *radius* hasn't increased the way it should have," Jožka clarified, pointing to the scale at the bottom of the image.

"Oh." Matt hadn't actually memorized how many arcseconds' wide the last Einstein ring had been, but someone had helpfully added a mark to the scale that showed it for comparison. The ring had only grown by about 60 percent in the fifteen months since the previous lensing. "That's not confusing," he said. "It's impossible." The square of the radius was supposed to be proportional to the black hole's mass divided by its distance. If the trajectory computed from the first two sightings was even remotely correct, the size of the ring should have more than doubled.

"They've thrown the engines into reverse," Aaron joked. "They don't like what they've seen, and now they're plotting a course for home."

Yuki said, "If only."

Arun slapped his palms together in a sudden epiphany. "It's a second black hole!" he declared. "The one we saw in the first two lensings must have a lighter companion!"

Jožka snorted. "More likely someone hacked the telescope's software."

"No, Taraxippus is a binary," Arun insisted. "Nothing else makes sense."

"So how did these two black holes hook up?" Jožka challenged him. "The heavier one can't be more than a tenth the sun's mass, or we would have seen bigger shifts in the outer planets by now. Black holes that small can't form from stars. So what are the odds of two of them being squeezed into existence side by side in the Big Bang?"

"I'm not a cosmologist," Arun protested. "But apart from putting limits on the total population, I've never heard anyone seriously claiming to have pinned down anything about primordial black holes. Maybe they weren't just spread out at random. If they were born in clusters, it wouldn't be that strange if a lot of them ended up in pairs."

Matt was still too bewildered to take sides, but if these were the only choices, he knew which one he'd prefer.

The idea that anyone would mess with the observatory's software was disturbing, but if Taraxippus was replaced by a pair of Taraxippoi, all the past predictions based on a solo interloper would be rendered void, and all the new ones would be plagued by much greater uncertainty. Better to have some clown in an fsociety mask show up in a clip on the telescope's hard drive, boasting that they did it for the lulz, and offering to unlock the real data in exchange for ten of their least favorite world leaders wrestling each other in pig manure in the middle of Times Square.

The console chimed: another link had come through. Apparently the Hubble had received a tip-off from Chile when the lensing began, and now its own independent sighting had been analyzed. The ring really was smaller than it had any right to be. What's more, comparing the two views of the event from slightly different perspectives put bounds on the distance to whatever it was that had bent the starlight this time—placing it a little closer than the point Taraxippus would have reached if the old calculations had been reliable. Nothing had slowed down or retreated, and the black hole responsible for the first two lensings could not have magically shed mass.

Jožka turned to Arun. "Okay, I give up. It's a binary."

Matt said, "JPL will run new models. I bet there'll be something in an hour or two."

Aaron was mystified. "It'll take their computers *an hour*?"

"No, but they're not going to put anything onto the web without a few humans checking that it makes sense." Matt had been a student when the first tiny discrepancies began appearing in the orbits of Saturn and Uranus, and a paper rushed out by a prestigious journal had claimed the results as evidence for a long-hypothesized trans-Neptunian planet. But while other groups had failed to reach the same conclusion, it had taken a year for the authors of the original paper to identify the error in their own analysis and admit that something else entirely was frightening the horses.

Aaron tapped on his phone, then showed the result to Yuki. "*New Scientist* is reporting that the two black holes could be linked by a quantum wormhole!" he announced.

Jožka was unimpressed. "And . . . ?" Matt was fairly sure that whatever Alice and Bob might learn by dropping entangled qubits into a pair of black holes, current technology offered no more chance of making the thought experiment real than it did of grabbing both holes and tossing them back into the void.

Aaron shrugged and slid his thumb over the screen. "*The Guardian* says we missed the second black hole because the failure to decolonize astronomy left us with a dearth of observatories for the southern skies. But *The Australian* blames 'climate-change alarmists' for browbeating academics into cultish conformity that kept them from questioning the status quo. And *The Daily Mail* . . . oh, that's the same as *The Australian*, word for word, but they've put their own byline on it."

Matt gritted his teeth. "Is it too much to wait an hour for some facts?"

But Aaron was still intent on his feed. "Some dude on Reddit's running a poll on a name for the new black hole; it's got about ten K votes already."

Matt left and went to the mess. It was only half past ten, but he'd had breakfast at five. He made a salad of carrots and lettuce from the garden, then microwaved a potato. He opened the freezer and stared at the rows of dead-eyed fish, then closed it again. It wasn't just that he was sick of the taste; it was being so intimate with the cobias' own writhing breakfast.

Arun walked in just as Matt was sitting down to eat, and grimaced at the bland meal. "You really need to raid my stash," he said.

"I don't want to start relying on it. Isn't that what you said yourself?"

"I changed my mind. What's the point of having it, if we don't use it?" Arun fetched a small jar of some aromatic condiment and spooned a dollop onto the potato. Matt tried the result.

"Okay, now I'm an addict."

Arun sat down and ran a hand worriedly over his beard. "This is going to widen all the error bars, isn't it? While turning all the bad things bimodal."

"Yeah."

"Just when I was getting used to the old odds. There was just enough chance of things going badly that I didn't feel foolish being out here, but not enough to really lose sleep over it."

Matt said, "I always lost sleep."

"Really?" Arun was surprised. "At one in five hundred?"

"I don't think I ever took that at face value," Matt admitted. "I could follow all the modeling, and check the calculations . . . but how do you know there isn't something else you're missing?" In his own field, plucking failure rates out of a theoretical model without adding a hefty margin of pessimism would send you straight to hell, but if orbital mechanics was infinitely more pristine than anything involving fractures or corrosion, apparently it could still come up with a surprise or two. Especially when the bodies in question were invisible most of the time.

Matt was cleaning up when he heard Arun's phone beep.

"JPL have spoken," Arun said.

"So let's go take a look."

When they reached the control room, Jožka had brought up a map of the solar system, over which was superimposed a kind of landscape of probabilities for the points where either black hole might cross the plane of the ecliptic. Matt had been expecting two reasonably sharp, distinct peaks, but the uncertainties were now so great that there was just a huge elliptical mound that stretched all the way from Saturn's orbit to Venus's. The segment of Earth's orbit that it would occupy during the window for the crossing lay entirely within the mound.

"They really didn't need to draw a diagram," Yuki decided. "Eight words would have covered it."

Arun took the bait. "Eight words?"

"We might be fine. We might be fucked."

Aaron laughed nervously. "So if we're Noah's Ark now, where are the giraffes?"

Matt said, "By the time of the crossing there'll be thousands of arks at sea. With this news, maybe tens of thousands. There are people who were planning to take seed banks, and DNA collections, and even frozen animal embryos. So relax, Shem, it's not all down to us." He felt calm as he spoke the words, as if this earnest collective effort really would offer anyone the least bit of comfort if the tides rose up and drowned the coastlines.

"Seriously, though . . . what if my parents . . . ?" Aaron's voice faltered.

"We can phone them," Yuki said quietly. "They can join us, if that's what they decide."

Matt looked away, trying to respect their privacy, but he understood what it would be like to struggle with the implications of the offer. Of course Aaron wanted his family to be safe—but to truly believe that the only safe place for them was a berth at sea, he'd also have to believe that millions of other people might die.

5

"There's not that much looting," Selena declared. "And the shops have only run out of a couple of things. Long-life milk has gone entirely black market. I mean, really? I would have thought coffee, or toilet paper."

"Why do you keep downplaying it?" Matt replied, shifting his phone to his left hand so he could wipe the sweat from his right palm.

"I'm not!" she insisted. "People have had a couple of years to stockpile whatever they wanted, even if they thought the chance of anything happening was minuscule. The only ones who haven't done that are temperamentally incapable of entertaining the possibility of disaster, and nothing they've heard in the last few days is going to change their minds."

Matt had seen images of traffic jams visible from space, where cities whose residents had some memory of flooding—and the means to act on it—had headed inland en masse. But Perth was not New Orleans, and apparently even the beachside suburbs were only half empty.

"If you don't want to come out to the *Mandjet*, at least

get away from the coast. Take Mum and Dad on a road trip somewhere. I'm pretty sure they've never seen Uluru."

Selena hesitated. "All right. I'll talk to them."

Matt said, "If a tidal bulge comes sweeping in . . ."

"I know," she replied. "But they're more worried about people looting the house, or not being around to protect things from the water if there's a smaller flood."

"Tell them you'll buy them new carpets, if it comes to that."

"I'll find a way to convince them," she promised.

Matt wanted to insist that she go alone if her powers of persuasion failed her, but he knew he'd be wasting his breath. If their parents stayed, she would stay and look after them. It was what he would have done himself, if she hadn't been there.

"Call me when you've talked to them," he said.

"All right."

Matt left his cabin and walked out onto the deck, hoping to catch the afternoon breeze. Up ahead, Aaron was standing by the rail, holding his phone by his side.

Matt approached him. "Any luck?"

"No." Aaron's face flushed with embarrassment. "They think a passing black hole is more likely to suck a boat into the sky, than a house with good foundations."

Matt said, "Tell them that if *anything* flies into the sky, it will mean one of the holes has come close enough to strip away half the atmosphere, then toss the Earth out past the orbit of Pluto. Hiding in the storm cellar with Aunt Em won't save them."

"Are you sure we're not more vulnerable at sea, though?" Aaron asked. "If a mountain of water appears on the horizon—"

Matt cut him off. "If a mountain of water appears, it will be as wide as the Indian Ocean, so out here we won't even notice the slope. The danger comes when water's forced to move through narrow gaps, or over a shallow sea floor. So the best place to be if things go tidal is in deep water that will stay deep, or on dry land far enough from the coast to stay dry."

"I tried to persuade them to go out into the desert," Aaron replied. "But they said they're not moving unless the government tells them to."

"That's never going to happen," Matt predicted. "If they made it the official line, and people acted on it, every inland town would have its population quadrupled. No one's going to die from sleeping outdoors in this weather, but what happens with food, water, sanitation?"

Aaron groped for a solution. "There must be army engineers . . . ?"

"Yeah, and I'm sure they could cope with a few thousand civilians, in one or two locations. They could truck in water and dig latrines. But if every coastal city was evacuated, it would be a public health disaster. If the government had prepared for the worst from the start, and gambled a few billion dollars on it, they could have been in a position to do something useful. But at this point . . ."

Matt trailed off. He had trouble summoning up any real sense of disappointment; it had been clear for a while that the bets were being placed very differently.

Yuki joined them. Matt gave her a questioning look.

"My family's heading out of Osaka," she said. "They have relatives in a small village in the mountains. A lot of their neighbors will be doing the same."

"Will the villages cope?"

Yuki shrugged. "Civil defense are doing something with ration packs and chemical toilets. I don't know where they'll put everyone, but at least they can melt snow for drinking water if they have to."

Arun appeared, beaming.

"Someone waiting at the marina?" Matt asked hopefully.

"No, but they've agreed to go inland. If you seriously thought my parents would ever set foot on this malodorous pool noodle, you clearly haven't spent enough time with them."

Matt spread his arms resignedly. "And there I was ready to put chocolates on their pillows."

Jožka showed up, looking bemused. "They're taking a

holiday back to Brno," she announced. "My whole family's going to stay with my grandparents for a couple of months. They were begging *me* to join *them*!"

"Well, Brno's a long way from the sea," Yuki conceded. "And the food's sure to be nicer than ours."

"No love for the *Mandjet* anywhere," Arun lamented.

"Do you want me to talk to your parents?" Matt asked Aaron. "I'm no expert on black holes, but marine engineers know a lot about tides, and there's a chance I can sell them on a holiday in the gold fields just by wearing them down with my extensive knowledge of the local amphidromic system."

Aaron nodded and raised his phone to call the number. As Matt prepared to make his pitch, he tried to damp down his own sense of the true scale of the problem. He needed to make the trip sound as unremarkable as leaving town to avoid an uncomfortable summer. No one waited for official directions to do that, or bogged down in a moral quagmire if their neighbors chose not to follow them. Disasters belonged to distant places, or bad movies, but maybe people could still be persuaded to act if it made them feel . . . not even *safe*—which raised the stakes too high by invoking thoughts of the opposite state—but merely *prudent*.

6

Matt lay awake for hours, floating in a haze of weariness and unwanted vigilance, willing his phone to beep to put an end to the waiting, then cursing his impatience and begging it to stay silent instead.

When he did sleep, he dreamed of Einstein rings—and in the morning he woke to find them everywhere: in the stain left on the table by the bottom of his coffee mug, in the sunlight reflected from a can onto the wall. But not on the control room console. Not yet.

There had to come a point when the sluggish motion of the Taraxippoi across the sky was replaced by a sudden rush, like a train rattling by—and the longer it took for this oncoming train to appear to veer sideways, the closer that placed the Earth to the tracks. If you were waiting for a sign that the headlights were no longer bearing down on you, no news was bad news.

But when the train was invisible, the cues weren't so easy to read. As the black holes swept past new stars whose light might fall under their sway, the chance of another lensing on any given day depended on the speed at which they crossed the sky *now,* not how far they'd come from the start—and while an object approaching almost head-on seemed frozen in place at first, by the time it shot past it could only appear faster, by virtue of its proximity, than if it had had more leeway. The quirks of the lensing process exacerbated the effect, switching the silence from ominous to auspicious even sooner—though like everything else, the actual timing depended on quantities still unknown.

Matt had worked through all the calculations, but he still didn't know what to wish for: an early detection to end the uncertainty, or one that came so late that the world was a quivering mess before the verdict arrived—declaring that everything had been fine all along.

. . .

Selena sent Matt a picture of their parents at a camping ground near Leonora. He couldn't tell from the tight shot of the tent if the place was crowded or deserted, but he took Selena's upbeat message at face value: "Having a great time out here. Phone coverage patchy, but can't believe there are so many stars."

Aaron's mother turned out to have a welcoming cousin in Cobar, a small mining town in New South

Wales six hundred kilometers from the coast, and from what Matt heard the place had hardly been besieged. Arun's family had chosen Roma in Queensland, for reasons that weren't entirely clear, and booked into a hotel. Yuki's family reported crowding in the village, but no panic or privation, and in Brno the locals were apparently describing the influx as "no worse than the tourist season." But footage from the wider world spanned everything from evacuees crowding into school gymnasiums to scenes of chaos and hostility at borders, desperation in makeshift displacement camps, and sheer fatalism where poverty and geography left people with no choice but to stay put.

Matt walked past the empty cabins of his ark, ashamed at the waste but at a loss to find a remedy. He tried calling his friend Eduardo in Dili, just to be sure he'd had no trouble getting his family up into the hills, and the failure of the call to connect made him hopeful that they'd succeeded.

He sent a message to Samira, the last in the line of ex-girlfriends who'd reached the conclusion that, between the rigs and the construction of the *Mandjet,* he had no time for anything else. He had expected to be rebuffed swiftly, so he took heart from the silence as he pictured her calmly weighing up her options. After two days, though, he realized that she wasn't going to reply at all.

"Did you ever think of inviting Carol?" he asked Arun.

"I texted her last week," Arun confessed. "She told me to fuck off and stop gloating."

"Were you gloating?"

Arun took out his phone and read what he'd sent. "'Hope you're okay with all this craziness. Plenty of free berths here for you and your family if you want them.'"

Matt shook his head reprovingly. "You monster."

Arun wasn't taking it personally. "I guess when the world's falling apart, the last thing anyone wants is to be stuck on a boat with their ex."

Matt said, "That's probably true, but I'm starting to think it's even simpler than that."

"Simpler how?"

"When the world's falling apart, the last thing anyone wants is to be stuck on a boat, period."

• • •

Matt was still awake when the alert came through from Siding Spring, around midnight. He was first to the control room, but he wasn't alone for long.

The new lensing was by Taraxippus A, the heavier member of the pair. The radius of the ring was eight arc-seconds, almost four times bigger than at A's last sighting—putting it sixteen times closer. Maybe twice the distance between the

Earth and the sun.

Jožka said, "I used to think the solar system was too small a target for anything to hit by chance."

"Until Taraxippus?" Aaron assumed.

"No, until 'Oumuamua in 2017. That passed within twenty-four million kilometers of the Earth. One sixth the distance to the sun."

Aaron grunted with surprise; maybe he'd missed the news at the time. "What would happen if Taraxippus A came that close?"

Yuki said, "Tides of maybe four or five meters. Not trivial, but not apocalyptic."

"Okay." Aaron smiled, as if taking both the precedent and the hypothetical consequences to heart. Matt was tempted to point out that the tides themselves might turn out be the least of their worries, but he bit his tongue; there was no point quibbling over details until they knew what was actually in store.

The Hubble reported a follow-up sighting, and though the parallax couldn't really pin down the distance, it put it within the expected range, proving that at least things were making sense now without recourse to ever more epicycles.

They waited for JPL to recompute the trajectories. Matt knew of a dozen other groups who might post their results earlier, but none of them had a rendezvous with Pluto on their CV and, if anything, their haste inspired less confidence.

When the analysis finally came through, the mound of possibilities had contracted at the edges, but it remained dismayingly broad.

"Hooray, Venus is spared!" Jožka proclaimed sarcastically.

"How can this not have helped?" Aaron protested.

Matt said, "It's helped, but they've still only had four observations in total. Give them a few more—"

"A *few*?" Aaron looked around angrily, as if he'd been lured here under false pretenses.

Yuki took his arm. "It won't be much longer now. The lensings will come faster. Soon we'll know exactly where these things are going, how heavy they are, and what the damage will be."

Aaron was not placated. "A month ago, no one even knew *how many* there were!"

"Well, that's progress right there," Arun said amiably. "Seriously, they're too close to hide now. They won't be able to move without giving themselves away... and they don't have any choice about moving."

"You people are full of shit," Aaron muttered. He pulled free of Yuki and walked out.

Jožka turned to Yuki. "What did we do?"

Yuki shook her head. "Nothing. But we've been thinking about this stuff for years, and he hasn't—so he's coming at it with different expectations."

Matt pressed the heel of his palm against his eyes. "If we're lucky, there'll be sightings around the clock now, so we'd better make a habit of grabbing some sleep in between."

As they left the control room, Jožka had an idea. "Next time, let's just say that it's like an election night. When only four seats have been counted, no one really knows if it's the end of civilization. If you want certainty, you have to wait for the numbers."

• • •

Matt woke to find his stomach knotted and his body bent against a constant dull cramp. But he went through the motions of ordinary activities, glad of the work roster to tell him what to do. Shoveling maggots and spreading manure in the garden did nothing to occupy his mind, but despite the discomfort it still felt far better than lying on his bunk, half dreaming, juggling scenarios for the future that he had no power to summon into being or dispel.

The next lensing came in the early afternoon, spotted first in Chile. The mound of uncertainty shrank a little more, almost ruling out a direct hit on the Earth.

An actual collision had always been stupendously unlikely, but now that it lingered on the margins Matt couldn't help feeling a compulsive need to see it decisively ruled out. Never mind that it would have been mercifully swift compared to the prolonged agony of any kind of near miss; the idea offended his whole sense of how the universe should work. If 'Oumuamua and its successors had made the solar system seem more like a full-sized dartboard than the eye of a needle, the Earth itself was still orders of magnitude smaller, to the point where a bull's-eye could only imply either comic-book aliens using black holes as weapons—behavior so cheesy it would be embarrassing to share the galaxy with them—or the cruelest of coincidences for an event so improbable to befall, not a barren planet, but one bearing life.

A day later, Mauna Kea granted him his wish, trimming the possibilities more than enough to guarantee that the Taraxippoi would not strike any planet. And in the wake of the sixth lensing, the crossing points for the two holes formed discernible peaks on the map, overlapping in the foothills but no longer merging into a single plateau.

As Matt stared bleary-eyed at the console, he noticed a short line of text below the map. JPL had been making predictions for the next lensing event each time, usually with fairly low confidence levels, but the line now read: "Tarax-ippus A / HIP 33008 (magnitude 7), 6 Feb 15:37–15:52 UTC, R_E = 8.5 arc-seconds, likelihood 75%."

He pointed to the most unexpected feature. "Magnitude seven! Not naked eye, but bright enough for binoculars. Except . . . eight point five arc-seconds? That's too small to see any kind of ring."

Jožka slapped him gently on the side of the head. "Is there anyone still in there, or have you left us completely?"

"What?" Matt thought for a moment, then groaned at his stupidity. "Okay, sorry. We should still see the brightening. Assuming it's dark here." He cowed away from Jožka's hand. "That's really not helping." He struggled to recall the time difference, then announced, "Tomorrow night, just before midnight."

* * *

Matt lay down on his bunk without much hope of sleep, but he set an alarm anyway. He dreamed that he was back on the rig in the Timor Sea, roused by the shrill of a Klaxon—but he knew for a fact that it was only a drill, measuring the time it took for everyone to evacuate. As he clambered down the ladder, Eduardo, coming after him, checked his watch and called down amiably, "Hey Matt, didn't your contract expire a year ago? You can't use the lifeboats if you're not on the payroll."

He staggered to his feet and shut off the alarm. His mouth was dry and his eyelids felt like sandpaper. He turned on the light, splashed water on his face, and forced himself to stand upright.

Everyone was gathered on the deck outside the control room. Aaron had stayed away from the last few lensings, but Yuki must have talked him halfway out of his defensive sullenness. Matt was still feeling angry himself that waking life had reasserted its primacy, but this might be the closest any of them came to directly perceiving the Taraxippoi, and he wasn't going to miss the chance to tell his grandchildren about it.

Yuki had brought the binoculars; Matt waited his turn for a prelensing inspection. Sirius was easy to find, almost directly overhead, and Matt knew the star they wanted was about ten degrees south, but it took a while for him to steady the view by counter-swaying his body, and then a minute or two more talking it over with his crewmates—comparing memories of the map they didn't dare consult again, lest they lose their dark-adaptation—before he was sure he knew what he was looking at, and would notice if it changed. HIP 33008 was an insignificant gray speck, invisible to all the old civilizations that might have given it a more memorable label, and the only way Matt could fix his attention on it was through its relationships with half a dozen more luminous neighbors.

Arun said, "There's got to be at least a hundred million people watching this." He gestured to the north. "Most of east Asia, if the skies are clear and the city lights don't ruin it."

"They're switching off the streetlights in Shanghai," Aaron replied.

"There had better be a show, then," Matt decided. If this one prediction was borne out, verified firsthand by millions of witnesses, the astronomers would win back a lot of confidence with the public—and once the trajectories were completely nailed down there would be a lot less room for random idiots to insist that they knew better than any so-called expert.

"Eleven thirty-seven P.M.," a bland synthetic voice intoned. Jožka had set her phone to speak the time on the minute.

Yuki had the binoculars; she raised them and stood swaying for ten or fifteen seconds, then announced, "No change yet," before passing them on to Aaron. Matt hadn't expected anything so soon; even if the prediction was perfect, the brightness would only rise slowly at first, as Taraxippus A came closer to the line of sight to the star.

Five minutes into the nominal lensing period, Jožka said, "Okay, that's different. It's almost as bright now as the one to the west of it." By the time Matt got his hands on the binoculars, her claim seemed like an understatement; HIP 33008 was outshining that guide star. And he was sure that the speck had grown enlarged and distorted, even if its detailed shape was beyond the limits of his acuity.

He passed the binoculars to Arun, who muttered something so softly that Matt couldn't make out the words, but the tone came so close to echoing his own tentative mixture of delight and terror that it made the hair stand up on his arms. *They were standing here joined by nothing but light and glass to a black hole.* No billion-dollar telescopes with their arrays of sensors, no internet, no screens. There it was, right above them, closer than Jupiter ever came, closer than Mars when it was far.

Matt's chest tightened. He wanted to weep, but he felt too self-conscious, and he was afraid of smearing the lenses when the binoculars came back to him. When they did, his eyes were clear, but the star seemed to blur and shimmer as it outshone all the drab neighbors he'd once needed as landmarks just to find it.

When he passed the binoculars to Arun again, and

glanced up unaided, he realized that he could now see the star easily with his naked eye. Or rather, *the curved space around the black hole* was acting as a better lens than the glass ones he'd set aside, and what it lacked in sharpness of focus it more than made up for in size.

The five of them stood in silence, listening to the waves and the machinery of the *Mandjet*, watching the star brighten and fade. When it disappeared from view, no one felt the need to use the binoculars again.

Jožka said, "Maybe in a few years we can send a probe to chase after them, and finally test all the theories to our hearts' content."

Yuki smiled. "That would be wonderful."

"I think this trumps my father seeing Halley's Comet," Arun decided. "He always made a big deal about that."

Matt said, "Time for the lensing party." Whatever the event might turn out to have revealed about their future, he wanted to hold on a little longer to the thing itself.

Aaron and Yuki had brought a case of beer with them when they came on board, but apparently that was long gone, so everyone went to the mess and gorged themselves on the last of the jalebi, washing it down with strong, unsweetened black tea until they were bloated.

Jožka sighed contentedly and massaged the side of her

jaw. "That's two cavities at least, but it was worth it."

Arun said, "I think you've just invented a new food rating scheme, but it could do with some refinement. Do you mean two fillings, two root canals, or two extractions?"

There was a brief cacophony as everyone's phones buzzed and beeped, not quite all at once and with different choices of alert tones.

In the control room, the map from JPL was waiting for them on the console. The landscape had shrunk to two tiny blobs: Taraxippus A and B at their closest approaches to the Earth, pinned down to within a few thousand kilometers. The heavier hole would come first, on 16 March, and the lighter one three days later.

"Seventy-two million kilometers for A, seventy-five for B," Jožka read.

Aaron gave a strangled cheer that turned into a sob. "That's nothing!" He looked to Yuki for confirmation. "Inverse cube law makes that eight times stronger than the solar tides, but these fuckers weigh ten times less, so that brings it down to less than solar."

Yuki embraced him. "That's right, babe."

Matt closed his eyes and tried to share in their jubilation. The millions of people who'd stayed by the shores would not drown, or face a crushing exodus in the scrabble to find higher ground. He should have felt ecstatic.

But if seventy million kilometers was more than enough to rule out a Biblical deluge, he'd seen too many simulations not to dread what was coming next, in the fine print.

When he opened his eyes, Jožka's finger was poised to tap a link in the corner of the screen, but she'd been waiting for everyone to signal their readiness.

He said, "Go ahead."

The second map showed the Earth's new orbit in the aftermath of the encounter, overlaid on the old one. The Taraxippoi would not have time to drag the planet far from its current position, so the two curves continued to pass through almost the same point in mid-March, and six months later in mid-September. The black holes wouldn't even change the Earth's speed much: most of the deceleration induced by the tug of their gravity as they approached from behind would be regained once they overtook the planet and began to pull it forward instead.

What they would do, though, as they passed by on the outer side of the orbit, was turn the Earth's velocity vector to point a little farther away from the sun. And by forcing it to veer off the road this way they were letting it do all the damage itself: the effect of that slight change in direction would build up over time, long after they were gone. So although the old and new orbits agreed in

March and September, in June the planet would be 7 percent farther from the sun, and in December 10 percent closer.

Aaron spent a minute parsing the new map, but it was well-annotated, so there wasn't much chance of misreading it. "Our summers get hotter, and our winters colder. Right?"

Matt said, "Yes."

"And the opposite in the northern hemisphere," Aaron reasoned. "But by how much?" Yuki must have taught him how to calculate the tides, but apparently she'd spared him the Stefan-Boltzmann law.

Jožka said, "It's going to take some serious climate modeling to answer that properly, but as a crude rule of thumb you can halve the fractional change in the distance and apply it to the Earth's average temperature above absolute zero, which is two hundred and ninety degrees. So maybe ten degrees Celsius colder in June, and fifteen degrees warmer in December."

Aaron nodded soberly. "All right. So . . . five degrees warmer on average?"

Matt said, "I think you mean two and a half, but it will probably be a bit less, on average. We speed up when we're closer to the sun, so we spend more time farther away."

"Okay. Two degrees, then?"

"That sounds right," Matt conceded. "But remember, it's just an average."

Aaron was undaunted. "We *knew* two degrees was coming down the track! So maybe now that it's happening earlier, that will motivate people to get serious. This could be a good thing, in the long run. The Ghost of Climate Future to shake us up before it's too late!"

Matt glanced at Yuki, wondering if he should leave it to her to break the news gently, but he couldn't see how it would help to drip-feed the unpleasantness.

He said, "This is not going to be the same as two degrees of global warming. Our summers will be hotter, our winters will be colder—they're not going to split the difference. And when it's fifteen degrees hotter in December—which means ten in some places, and twenty in others—the fact that it's colder in June won't help; most things that break from one extreme are not going to repair themselves when they're slammed just as hard in the opposite direction. Crops are going to fail, forests will die, reefs will vanish, fisheries will collapse . . . and not by the end of the century. Some within a decade. Some within a year."

Aaron went quiet, and Matt felt a twinge of guilt for speaking so bluntly. But if they'd been spared the horror of a tidal inundation that might have killed half a billion people in a day, the only real reprieve would come if they wasted no time preparing for the slow motion equivalent. From March, the Earth would be following a new path: that was beyond doubt now. And everyone needed to start looking for the best way to survive the change.

PART TWO

7

Matt arrived at the client's house just as the blizzard hit. He parked the van in the street and ran for the door, but even when he reached the veranda he found the wind blowing in on him obliquely, with gusts powerful enough to carry the lighter pieces of hail with it.

He rang the doorbell and waited, hunched into his jacket. An elderly man opened the door a crack.

Matt shouted over the wind, "Mr. Carmichael?"

The man nodded and motioned him in; Matt squeezed through into the hall.

"I thought you'd cancel the job, in this weather," Mr. Carmichael said.

"I can still do the ceiling insulation," Matt assured him. "The double glazing and the lagging for the water pipes might have to wait."

"The pipes burst this morning! I'm going to have to get a plumber in."

"I'm sorry to hear that." Matt followed him through the house to the laundry, where the hatch to the ceiling was located, and where the supplier had left the insulation panels stacked against the wall. "I'll just get my ladder from the van."

"No, I've got one in the garage." Mr. Carmichael gestured at a side door. "Just through there. It'll save you going outside again."

"Thank you."

Up in the roof space, the wind rattled the tiles and insinuated itself through the gaps between them to crisscross the gloom with unpredictable planes of icy air. But the job itself was routine; there were no exposed electrical wires, and no halogen lamps in the ceiling to set fire to anything that trapped their heat. Without Arun helping it took twice as long to maneuver each panel through the hatch, but Matt lost himself in the work and treated the wind as background music. Ninety minutes later, he was done.

"Can I get you a cup of tea?" Mr. Carmichael offered as Matt folded the ladder. "I still have plenty of water; I filled up some containers before I shut off the mains."

Matt glanced out the window; he had no more appointments until the next day, and it probably wasn't safe yet on the roads.

"Thanks, that's kind of you."

They sat at a table in the kitchen. "Are you on your own here?" Matt asked. It was a huge house, with at least four bedrooms.

"My wife died last year."

"I'm sorry. Do you have any family around?"

"My daughter's overseas." Mr. Carmichael frowned, perhaps taking the question as a slight on his independence. "The weather's going to be a nuisance, but people have lived with winters like this for centuries, in other places: Manitoba, Mongolia. And they're saying the summer won't be much worse than it used to be in Kuwait."

Matt hoped that would be true. "Do you know what the temperature is right now in Dili?"

Mr. Carmichael shook his head. Matt didn't either, but when he took out his phone the answer didn't disappoint him. "Twenty-two degrees," he read. "With light rain clearing."

"Sounds nice, but in six months it will be a bit of a sauna, won't it?"

Matt said, "To put it mildly." He hesitated, unsure of the signals he was getting, but he pressed ahead. "Have you heard of the Seasonal Sharing Scheme?"

"No."

"If you sign up, you get to spend your winters with a family in the tropics, where it's likely to be balmy. Then in the summers you host the same family down here—where it won't be pleasant, but at least it's survivable with aircon."

Mr. Carmichael said, "I've heard of *that,* but I thought

it was closed now. I mean, you could fit all of Darwin and Townsville into the spare rooms of Sydney, so it's no surprise they got more offers than they needed."

Matt suspected that the government subsidy also helped, but it seemed uncharitable to mention that. "The in-country scheme is booked out," he agreed, "but I'm talking about people in the countries to the north. PNG, East Timor, Indonesia."

"I thought they were going to China."

"China's taking some seasonal migrants, but it's hardly got room for everyone."

"Well, nor have we. Isn't there some quota that the prime minister announced?"

Matt said, "Two hundred thousand people. But this would be on top of that."

"On top of it?" Mr. Carmichael eyed Matt leerily. "You're trying to find some kind of loophole?"

"The quotas are for permanent migrants," Matt explained. "With triple S, families just take turns hosting each other. No one gets new citizenship."

"So how would they support themselves here?"

"Employment, if possible. But we're hoping some people will be in a position to bring food with them—maybe nuts, legumes, that kind of thing. Agriculture's going to be crazy everywhere, but the equatorial zone might stay productive through the southern winter, when we sure as hell won't be growing anything outdoors." Matt looked to the window; the blizzard was showing no signs of abating. He took out a card. "Anyway, this is the website if you think you're interested."

He held the card out, but Mr. Carmichael didn't take it. Matt put it on the table and rose to his feet.

Mr. Carmichael said, "I'd rather know the contact details for your supervisor. I don't expect to get a political spiel from a government contractor."

"I'm sorry if I offended you." Matt had thought the man's demeanor had been cautious; he'd missed the slide into outright hostility. "But I'm not a government contractor, I'm a volunteer." The same federal scheme that sent out the insulation to every pensioner would also pay for tradespeople to come and install it, eventually, but it would probably have been September by the time that happened.

"So who's your supervisor?" Mr. Carmichael demanded.

"You are," Matt replied. "When I signed up on the website, the software checked my qualifications and police clearance; there are no other humans involved. If you want to give me a negative review, go ahead, but if you claim there's a problem with the installation, the system will send someone to check that." He walked into the hall. "I take it you don't want me back to do the glazing when the weather clears up, so I'll cancel that at my end so the site will let you submit a new request."

Outside, Matt sat in the van, waiting for the visibility to improve, wondering if it was worth giving in and paying black market prices for snow tires.

His phone beeped. It was the Insulation Army app, letting him know that he'd been suspended for "offensive language toward a client." He laughed wearily. He'd always hung up on cold-calling charities, so maybe this was his punishment for the hypocrisy of thinking he was entitled to ask people he'd never met to consider billeting strangers.

When the snow stopped falling and the wind died down, he drove home as slowly as a nervous L-plater, still wary of his limited experience with the road conditions. He found the house empty except for his mother in the kitchen, preparing dinner.

"Can I help with anything?" he asked.

"You could cut those up," she said, pointing to a collection of sickly vegetables she'd placed on the countertop.

Matt found a knife and started chopping. He hoped she wasn't just humoring him, making use of his stunted crop; since Selena had moved in the freezer was well-stocked, and even the current price of imported vegetables hadn't yet moved beyond reach of a lawyer's salary.

When his mother had no more jobs for him, he went

out to check on his Rube Goldberg greenhouse. The mesh screen that protected the wind turbine was glistening; it was steep enough that snow just slid off it, but it still acquired a fine coating of ice. Matt spent ten minutes scraping it with a wire brush; it wasn't worth wasting power on the heating element.

The building itself relied on more artificial heat and light than a Murmansk grow house, so he slipped inside as quickly as he could to avoid letting too much warmth escape. He hadn't been able to get hold of the same sensors Arun and Yuki had used for the *Mandjet*'s garden, so he had to inspect every plant by eye. But the weather seemed to have killed off every living creature in the air and the soil, and there was nothing left to either help or hinder his efforts. He might as well have been growing these carrots and eggplants in a cave on the moon.

When he returned to the house, Selena and his father were home, and everyone was about to sit down to dinner in front of the television news. The lead "story" was a propaganda piece: a government-supplied video showing off the billion dollars' worth of drones that the black-shirted goons of the Border Force had acquired to police the empty northern cities throughout the summer, lest anyone from closer to the equator creep in and find what would surely have been marginal respite. "The quotas we've set for climate migrants are the most generous in the world," the minister for Home Affairs read from her autocue. "But we cannot and will not allow our sovereignty to be undermined in the name of some false idea of compassion." When the speech moved on to hint at the need for vigilance against the risk of a military incursion, Matt struggled to keep himself from bursting out laughing. Most of the top brass in Southeast Asia had enriched themselves sufficiently to buy their way into Russia or China, but even the lower-ranked officers would have no reason to take the initiative. A soon-to-be-barren continent that barely stretched twenty degrees below the Tropic of Capricorn simply wasn't worth invading.

Everyone chewed their food in silence, until the stock market prices brought Matt's father to life. "See!" he crowed triumphantly. "It really didn't matter about the vineyard, in the end. Whatever we'd invested in, it would have tanked just the same."

"Except for snow tires," Matt suggested.

"What did Arun's parents invest in?" Matt's mother asked. "It must have done well, if they could afford new houses in Cairns and Launceston."

"They invested in being surgeons for thirty years," Matt replied. He glanced at Selena, hoping she might inject some sanity into the conversation, but she was lost in her own thoughts.

"They can't have just kept their money in the bank,

though. And if they'd put it into local real estate they would have lost it all."

"Do you want me to phone him up and ask?" Matt offered, deadpan.

His mother frowned. "No, I'm sure he's busy with the boat. But next time you're talking . . ."

Matt collected up the plates and took them to the kitchen so he could wash the dishes. He was pretty sure the family could survive the winter, with or without him. But if the summer went badly—if the city hit 60 degrees, desalination couldn't keep up with demand, and imported food became unaffordable or simply couldn't make it through the equatorial zone—then his presence alone would be useless. He couldn't jury-rig a suburban house into a self-sustaining space habitat, exploiting every ray of sunlight, recycling every drop of sweat. If the summer went badly, the only thing to do would be to get them all onto the *Mandjet.* And if he wasn't already on board himself, there'd be no guarantee it would be possible.

He went to his room and phoned Arun.

"How's Perth?" Arun asked.

"Siberian. Where are you now?"

"A bit south of Broome."

"Can you wait for me there? Just a day or two."

"Sure."

"I think I'll need to hitchhike. How are you guys doing?"

"Everything's fine. But the baby flies miss you so much."

"Fuck off." Matt found the Town Beach boat ramp on a map and sent the coordinates.

Arun said, "See you in a couple of days."

8

When Matt thanked the truck driver and walked into Broome, it looked as if someone had started to build a film set for a remake of *Bran Nue Dae,* then realized that shooting it in Winnipeg wasn't such a good idea. The trunks and branches of the dead palm trees and boabs might have been fiberglass props, waiting to have foliage glued on, and beneath the dull, overcast sky every building with a wide veranda or a touch of bamboo had the air of an impostor, desperately in need of some cinematic magic to make it more convincingly tropical. People walked the streets with their eyes cast down, wrapped up against the chill in repurposed clothing; Matt was quite sure that none of the scarves on view had started their lives that way. Maybe there'd be a few weeks in September when everyone could dress for the beach again, before they had to be bused south to escape the inferno.

His phone had had no signal since Carnarvon, but as soon as he had a clear view of the water he could see the *Mandjet* in the middle of Roebuck Bay, maybe a kilometer away. He thought of paying a local boat owner to ferry him out, but he decided to sit and wait for a while, and after an hour or so he spotted the runabout heading toward him.

"Welcome back!" Arun shouted as he approached the beach. "Third time lucky. I was starting to get worried."

Matt held his phone up and shook it. "Sorry."

The boat stopped in the shallows, and Matt waded out and clambered on board. Before he could say a word, Arun beamed at him and embraced him tightly. That wasn't usually his style; Matt couldn't recall the two of them actually hugging since they'd helped thrash the law students in a rugby match a decade ago.

"Is everything all right?" he asked.

"Absolutely." Arun kept smiling as he started up the outboard and set off for the *Mandjet*. Matt didn't push him for an explanation; under the circumstances, anyone who could keep from sinking into despondency was probably best left unquestioned, lest it break the spell.

In the shelter of the bay the water was calm, making the docking easy. They met up with the others in the mess. Matt had felt badly about leaving his crewmates to head north without him, however much they'd protested that they understood, and it was a relief to find no flickers of resentment on their faces at the prodigal's return.

"How's your family?" he asked Aaron, everyone else's being more or less out of harm's way.

"They decided to stay in Cobar," Aaron replied. "There's a plan to fit out the copper mine so the whole town can live down there for the worst parts of the year."

"That's ambitious." Matt had fantasized about digging a bunker in his parents' backyard, but the geology would not have been accommodating.

"I guess they'll be surviving on mushrooms," Aaron added. Matt wasn't sure if he was joking.

The five of them sat down together for a lunch of grilled fish. Matt took a bite and sighed. "Ah, there's that taste I've missed!" He was joking as he uttered the words, but there was something comforting in the constancy of the food supply that almost made up for the monotony.

When they'd finished eating, Jožka asked Matt, "Are you up for a meeting, or do you want to leave it till tomorrow?"

"No, I'm ready." On the long ride up the coast, Matt had contemplated trying to lobby people one-on-one before they made a decision on the *Mandjet*'s future, but he'd given up on the idea. He wasn't cut out for that kind of politicking, and it would be better if everyone just spoke their mind freely.

Yuki said, "If we're going to start offering a taxi service, we need to think about the routes that will be in high demand. Anyone who can't get into China overland will want to try their luck in the Pacific. But given that British

Columbia's already seeing boat arrivals from half of South America, avoiding the crowds will probably mean going all the way up to the Bering Sea."

"The Russian navy might have something to say about that," Jožka replied. "And the Americans, for that matter."

Aaron said, "Won't they be too busy with the Mexican border to care about Alaska?"

"They have enough guns to go around," Jožka remarked dryly. "Anyway, the whole idea that the Arctic is about to bloom is just misconceived. Sure, the sun's going to be brighter in winter, but if you're so far north that it's scraping the horizon the benefits won't be that great. And then the summer's *colder*. That's not a recipe for turning tundra into farmland."

"There are people talking seriously about building new islands in the North Pacific," Arun said. "There are dozens of guyots in the Emperor seamounts that aren't far from the surface. China has had plenty of experience turning submerged land into islands; it's about time they put it to good use."

Matt said, "That could take years."

"Sure," Arun agreed. "But if we can help people get closer to the region, at least it would mean that the host countries wouldn't have to absorb them all. They can be temporary residents, waiting for their own new nation to be completed."

Matt wasn't persuaded. "Don't you think China will have factored that in already? If they do start building islands, they'll have plenty of temporary residents of their own to populate them."

"Then someone else will have to build more," Arun countered. "The more refugees there are in the North Pacific rim, the more pressure there'll be to make homes for them."

Jožka said, "That's assuming they don't just sink the boats before anyone so much as sets foot on shore."

Arun went quiet. Jožka was sitting beside him; she reached up and put an arm across his shoulders in what looked like a conciliatory gesture, though it was not the kind of thing Matt had seen her do before.

He said, "If there's one shoreline worth reaching that no one's going to be defending with gunboats, it's not in the northern hemisphere at all."

Jožka smiled. "You want to do the southern loop?"

Matt nodded. "If we can make it work, wouldn't it be the safest choice?"

Yuki said, "The *Mandjet* can probably do it, but who's going to choose that kind of life, willingly? Eight months at home, two months at sea, two months in Antarctica. Where the climate will be lovely in summer, but there's no infrastructure, no one to trade with, and who knows what prospects for growing food?"

Matt laughed. "'Willingly'? I'm sure everyone would prefer their old lives back, but compared to a gulag on the Okhotsk Coast, I would have thought it sounded pretty good."

"The *Mandjet* could do it," Yuki repeated, "but what's the plan? We turn up in some Indonesian fishing village offering to take a few dozen people south? At which point we're outnumbered, and if they actually had their hearts set on the Pacific we won't be in a position to say no. But even if this is something people want, they're not going to want to do it alone—not in one vessel that holds less than a village worth of passengers."

"So we're part of a flotilla," Jožka interjected. "The more the better, if there's a problem at sea."

"How many fishing boats meant for short trips in an archipelago do you think could make it to Antarctica?" Yuki retorted. "If we're part of a flotilla, and the other boats just sink one by one, we'll have people piled up five-deep on every deck before we reach the Southern Ocean."

Matt said, "I have a friend in Dili, a marine engineer I worked with on the rigs. I want to ask him if he can figure out a way to use the *Mandjet* as a kind of hub. We can't take a huge number of passengers ourselves, but if Eduardo can pick the kind of boats that go with us, he's not going to choose anything that's likely to sink, and we can help out with food and drinking water so that everyone's provisions last longer. I mean, people are going to be doing this, with or without us. The question is: where would we be the most use? Trying to smuggle people to Alaska, when we're pretty much the slowest, least stealthy vessel on the ocean? Or keeping people fed, while moving fast enough for the temperature to stay comfortable for humans and cobia, in waters that no navy or coastguard will be trying to defend?"

Arun looked dismayed. "Once or twice, maybe it would work. But year after year? If we really want to help people, we should help put pressure on the countries to the north to make room for them, so they end up somewhere they can live a decent life."

Jožka said, "Whatever happens, China, Europe and North America aren't going to take everyone. Even if they wanted to, they don't have the capacity. Some people will have no choice but to find a way to keep living in the south. Maybe that means seasonal migration, maybe it means something else. I hope there are a hundred different solutions, but I can only think of one that the *Mandjet* could be part of."

They kept talking late into the afternoon. Matt couldn't allay all of Arun's and Yuki's qualms, but in the end they conceded that if there were people already committed to the southern loop, the *Mandjet* could play a role as a support vessel. Giving up hope of sanctuary in the north to try to roll with the climatic punches might or might not be a viable strategy, but having a supply of captive fish along the way could hardly make things worse.

When Matt stepped out onto the deck, the sky was black; however untropical the weather, the sun still sank as fast as ever. He hadn't actually spoken to anyone in Dili for almost a year; he hadn't wanted to sound out Eduardo prematurely only to find that no one else on the *Mandjet* agreed to the plan.

The call through the satellite triggered thirty seconds of buzzing and odd silences before the ringing started, but Eduardo answered almost at once. He greeted Matt cheerfully, though his voice sounded strained.

"How are you surviving the winter in Perth?" he asked. There was a baby crying somewhere nearby, and people shouting in the distance.

"Actually, I'm up near Broome," Matt replied. "Just off the coast."

"You're on a boat?"

"Remember that project I was working on in my spare time?"

Eduardo laughed. "How could I forget the *Mandjet*? You had more pictures of it than I had of my kids."

"It's finished now. Everything's working: the flies, the fish, the wave power."

"Congratulations. You stuck with that a long time."

Matt said, "So now that it's finished, the question is, what is it good for?"

He sketched the idea of the southern loop. When he stopped talking, Eduardo was quiet for so long that Matt began to wonder if he was struggling to find a way to let him down gently. The stakes were so high that everyone had started succumbing to wishful thinking, and there was no reason to think he was immune himself.

But when Eduardo finally spoke, he said, "This might be the push I need. I've been trying for months to get a fleet together to go south for the summer, but it's been hard to get anyone to make a commitment."

"So what are most people planning to do?" Matt asked.

Eduardo muttered something in Tetum that Matt was fairly sure was obscene. "Some people have been conned into paying smugglers who've promised they can get them into China. Some people think the whole thing's a conspiracy to get them off their land—they say the coming wet season will either be normal, or as cool as this dry season has been. And some people think they can tough it out, however high the temperature goes."

"But you've talked to people about Antarctica?"

"Of course. No one wants to do it, but some of my friends agree that it might be the least worst choice, compared to staying here and getting cooked, or being slaughtered by pirates off the coast of Mindanao."

Matt said, "Okay. So where do we go from here? Should I bring the *Mandjet* to Dili?"

"That wouldn't be so smart." Eduardo made it sound as if Matt had just proposed hang gliding into a volcano. "Everything's falling apart around here. If you sail that thing into Indonesian waters I promise you it will be in a scrapyard by nightfall."

"So . . . ?"

"Give me a chance to talk to people, then I'll get a group together to come and take a look. Maybe we can meet off Melville Island, but you shouldn't go farther north than that."

"All right."

When Matt hung up the call, he stood for a while, staring across the bay at the lights of Broome. He could hear music drifting over the water. As good as it felt to be vindicated, it would have been infinitely better to hear that everyone in Dili had a ticket to China, there was no need to flee into the wrong hemisphere entirely and he should stop thinking about Antarctica and go home and wait for life to return to normal.

9

The delegation approached in a battered wooden fishing boat, some twelve meters long. A mast rose from the deck, but it was a calm day and the sails were furled, leaving the boat chugging along on diesel.

The whole crew of the *Mandjet* had gathered to watch the arrival, passing around the binoculars and trying to read the name of the boat as they squinted against the glare of reflected sunlight, but the paint had flaked off to the point where any reconstruction would be pure guesswork. "Can you see that making it through the Roaring Forties?" Yuki asked.

Matt said, "No, but they're probably trying to keep a low profile. We're the ones auditioning for the trip."

When the boat pulled up beside the *Mandjet,* the sea was so quiet that Matt just lowered a ladder from the side of the deck, and four of the occupants in turn jumped to it and clambered up, leaving a teenage boy in charge at the wheel.

Eduardo introduced his companions, all weathered, silver-haired men: José, Martinho, and João. They shook hands with everyone, and thanked Matt in English when he said, "Welcome," but they left Eduardo to do most of the talking and translating. Matt had picked up a little Portuguese and Tetum from his fellow workers on the rigs, but not enough to speak without embarrassing himself.

Eduardo hadn't been entirely clear as to why the *Mandjet* had to pass muster with these particular people—whether it was a question purely of their status in the community, or more their expertise in maritime affairs. In any case, the guests were given a full tour, starting from the control room, taking in the garden and not shying away from the maggots. The four originators of the project had prepared short spiels on their areas of expertise: Jožka on the cobia, Yuki on the flies and the garden, Arun on the generators and electronics, Matt on the propulsion and the structure as a whole. Eduardo dutifully translated every word, but he seemed a bit bemused. "At least you didn't use PowerPoint," he whispered.

Matt wasn't sure how else the crew were meant to prove their competence; things had moved on since the days of the Great Nantucket Knot-Tying Contest. But however confident he was of the *Mandjet*'s capabilities, it was hard not to be intimidated by the weight of their guests' experience. And not just of the sea; these men were old enough to have lived half their lives under the Indonesian occupation, when a tenth of the country had died from starvation and violence. He felt as callow in their presence as the boy they'd left on the boat.

As the two groups stood on the deck looking inward, João asked through Eduardo, "How many adult fish are there, right now?"

"About twelve thousand," Jožka replied.

"How do you know that?"

"I do a rough census with sonar every week," she explained. "And some sample nettings to check their health and weight range."

João nodded thoughtfully, but then motioned toward the enclosure's inscrutable surface with an upturned hand. Matt wasn't sure what he was asking, but he seemed to take the lack of a reply as assent. He clambered over the rail and dived into the blue water, not bothering to shed his T-shirt.

He surfaced, took a breath, then submerged again. Matt wasn't sure why Jožka couldn't simply be taken at her word; what kind of scam could they be running that involved building a half-million-dollar aquaculture rig, but then only pretending to stock it?

It was at least a full minute before João appeared again, but he smiled and gave a thumbs-up to his associates. There were actual fish; this was not some stone soup trick where the *Mandjet's* crew lured people to Antarctica to do all the fishing for them.

"Are we getting closer?" Matt asked Eduardo.

"I'll let you know," he replied.

• • •

It was a week before Eduardo called. The connection was terrible, but Matt soon got the gist of the situation.

There were a number of coffee-growing families who'd expressed an interest in the trip south, but they were worried about the fate of their land if they left it unattended. If they came back to find that armed squatters had taken over the plantations, they weren't confident that the police, the courts, or any other branch of the government would still be strong enough to resolve the matter.

One solution to the impasse would be to go without those families. But not only would that mean the loss of the provisions they could bring, there was a doctor who had promised Eduardo that she would join the flotilla if, and only if, it comprised at least a thousand potential patients. Wherever that threshold had come from, she was adamant that if it wasn't met it would be her duty to remain on the island instead. Without the coffee farmers, the total fell short.

Matt was at a loss to suggest any strategy besides the obvious one. "Can't you tell these farmers that anyone who stays behind will be too busy trying to stave off heat-stroke to start making landgrabs?"

"They accept that it *might* be that bad, but they're not convinced enough to gamble on it," Eduardo replied.

"A doctor would be good," Matt conceded. "Can't the rest of us pitch in and just, you know . . . pay her?"

"I sounded her out on that, and it only made her more stubborn."

"So where does that leave us? Is this happening or not?"

Eduardo said, "I'll keep trying with the farmers. But if we don't get the doctor, a lot of other people might back out."

Matt took the news to the rest of the crew, who'd just finished lunch in the mess.

Yuki said, "Can't they put up an electric fence around their land? Solar-powered, with battery backup at night?"

Arun was skeptical. "It wouldn't be hard to tunnel under a fence, in four months. Or even just smash up the foundations and topple a section."

Aaron said, "Everyone's planning to evacuate Darwin, and they're not freaking out that their houses might be burgled."

"Most people aren't," Matt agreed, "but the government is freaking out on their behalf. Haven't you seen the drones?"

Aaron shook his head. "I'm too afraid to watch anything on the net in case I get beaten up for quota violations."

"You don't need the net," Matt replied. "We're close enough to Darwin that you can see them with binoculars."

Arun caught Matt's eye. He was frowning slightly, weighing something up before he spoke. Some technical quandary? Or a moral one?

Matt felt himself smiling before he was entirely sure that he'd correctly intuited the meaning, but then his uncertainty evaporated. "Fuck, yeah!"

Arun flinched a little, taken aback by his vehemence.

Jožka turned to Arun. "So what's the great idea?"

Arun looked to Matt, unsure now if they should put it into words.

Matt said, "Let me start by saying that if we end up in prison, I promise to install ceiling insulation and double glazing in all of your cells."

. . .

Matt leaned out the door of the control room and swept the binoculars along the horizon to the south, but all he could see was choppy blue-gray water meeting the bruise of distant thunderclouds.

"Nothing yet," he reported. He lowered the binoculars and stepped back into the room.

Arun turned away from the console, looking anxious now. "Maybe the signal's not strong enough." They'd tested it on one of the runabouts out to a distance of two kilometers from the *Mandjet,* but they didn't want to crank it up any higher lest they make problems for other boats.

"They might have varied the schedule," Jožka suggested. Over the past two weeks, they'd seen one of the drones make roughly the same surveillance sweep every morning and afternoon, day after day—but though the precise times and routes had varied, it was getting close to the end of the window within which the thing had usually passed through the circle that their signal ought to have reached.

"Maybe they changed the specs from the standard model," Arun fretted. "They could be doing something more elaborate, with a base station to supplement the satellites."

"What base station would it be using out here?" Matt wondered.

"Nothing's listed. But maybe they set one up, just for the drones."

Yuki said, "Wouldn't you have found it, when you swept the bands?"

"Not if they're restricting it for their own use. Without the right decryption key, it would just look like noise."

Matt could believe the private encryption part, but he was skeptical about anything so far offshore. A single GPS base station might cover a port or a harbor, but to cover the drones' flight path would take a few hundred of them, on anchored buoys spread across the Arafura Sea.

"If this thing's smart enough not to be fooled," Aaron began tentatively, "does that mean it's smart enough to know we're trying to fool it?"

"That's entirely possible," Arun confirmed glumly. "Goulburn super-max, here we come."

Jožka started kneading Arun's shoulders. Matt stepped out onto the deck and searched again.

"Forget Goulburn!" he called back. "The pizza's on its way."

Everyone ran out to join him, scrabbling for their turn with the binoculars. Matt was relieved, but the truth was they didn't quite have confirmation yet; the drone might have wandered closer to the *Mandjet* than usual just by chance, not because it thought it was somewhere else.

He returned to the control room and started up the

engines, leaving Arun on the deck with the binoculars.

"Go north!" Arun urged him.

Matt complied. This was going to be tricky; they needed to lure the drone farther off-course, without knowing its precise intended route in advance. In principle, it should be simple enough to gradually increase the distance between its true location and the one it was inferring from the fake GPS signals, but if the drone thought it was heading for point X, they needed to ensure that the point Y that it really was approaching wouldn't take it out of range of the *Mandjet's* transmitter.

A window on the console showed the fake coordinate grid overlaid on the real one, with the *Mandjet's* true position included, courtesy of the dead zone for the fake signal that had been shaped to include their own GPS receiver. The same map was being mirrored on Arun's phone, so he could fine-tune the divergence of the grids with a swipe of his thumb without even putting down the binoculars.

"Northeast!" Arun shouted. Matt turned the engines, almost wishing that they'd made everything portable enough to put on a runabout, purely for the sake of greater speed. But even if it was easier to chase the drone, it would have been harder to keep it in view from a low, unstable platform.

Over the next hour, they managed to keep up the dance: half shadowing the drone with the *Mandjet,* half tricking it into shadowing them back. Never going out of range, but never coming too close. Arun gradually slid the fake coordinate grid to the south; it was like slowly cranking an escalator in reverse, so a sufficiently dim robot would believe it was ascending what it took to be a stationary staircase much faster than it actually was.

"If it thinks it's over land, and it sees water . . ." Aaron mused.

"Then we're screwed." Matt doubted that their adversary could reliably distinguish a turtle from a gun, but even the trashiest image-recognition system could tell the difference between red dust, green vegetation, and blue water.

The drone was still heading fake-north, though, far from land, eager to scan the ocean for approaching vessels from Indonesia. It thought it was halfway to the Maluku Islands, when in truth it was farther east, and nowhere near that far north.

It was also skimming lower over the water than it realized. "My, what big waves you have, Grandma!" Matt joked in his best Bugs Bunny voice.

"Now you're getting creepy," Yuki replied.

"Sorry." But if the drone's algorithms were taking the

fake-GPS altitude seriously, they might well be logging reports of perilous seas.

"Okay, this is our best chance!" Arun decided. Matt cut the engines and headed out of the cabin with Jožka.

"Be careful," Arun urged her.

"Always."

She and Matt boarded separate runabouts and set out to meet the drone. It was gaining on the *Mandjet* now, but so low there was no chance of it seeing the craft. Matt slipped on an improvised balaclava, just in case he ended up in view; he glanced across the water and saw that Jožka was already wearing hers. If the drone's vision was being monitored in real time by a human, the ruse might soon be up, but he doubted that anyone was bothering; it wasn't a military device in a war zone, just an expensive stunt by the government's most profligate chest-beaters.

Arun brought the drone down as low as he dared: it looked like about six meters. Matt approached on the left, Jožka on the right. As they were about to pass it, they turned the boats around and started keeping pace with it, escorting it on either side.

Matt took the rope in his hands and looked to the side. Jožka nodded once, twice, thrice.

They threw their ropes together, aiming the loops at the curved feet of the landing frame. Jožka's hit its mark and she tightened it, but Matt's fell to the water. "Fuck." Jožka moved closer to the drone and played out some rope while Matt recovered and tried again. This time, he snagged the foot. He pulled back on the rope to secure the loop; he could feel the ratchets clicking. Then he heaved forty kilograms of ballast over the side of the runabout and it disappeared into the water, taking his rope with it.

Jožka gunned her motor and her runabout shot ahead. The drone plummeted, then hung a meter or so above the water like a strange parasailing robot, its four rotors struggling to keep it aloft against these inexplicable forces. But even as Jožka accelerated, it remained stubbornly airborne, refusing to be dunked. They'd misjudged the ballast.

Matt caught up with her and came alongside.

"I'm going in to try to weigh it down!" he shouted.

She hesitated for a moment, then nodded assent.

"On three, cut your motor for twenty seconds, then straight ahead as fast as you can!"

Matt counted, shut off his own outboard, then dived into the water. He wished he'd brought goggles, but he could see sunlight penetrating the green haze below the rolling surface. He swam a few strokes, reluctant to surface just to orient himself, then he spotted the silhouette of the vertical rope ahead. He propelled himself forward, unsure how much time had passed, and managed to grab the rope half a second before Jožka reached twenty.

As he ascended the rope, he felt its aerial support drop a little, but he was so buoyant himself that the change was probably all down to Jožka. The drone would almost certainly be raising alarms now, sending a distress signal to a satellite.

He broke the surface and reached for the landing frame, failed, climbed farther up the rope, then managed to grab hold of the metal. As he hoisted himself up, unsupported by the water now, the drone tipped and part of it entered the ocean.

The rotors weren't submerged, but they stopped spinning immediately. Matt waited cautiously for half a minute or so to see if they'd restart, then he clambered up past them and perched between the photovoltaic panel and the satellite antenna. Arun had sworn that the thing could survive hours of immersion without damage, but they needed to sever communications as rapidly as possible. Even with Matt's weight centered, the rotors shut off and the ballast pulling down, the thing had enough buoyancy not to go fully beneath the waves. But as water sloshed around Matt's knees, he scooped handfuls into the small dish antenna, hoping that would be enough to silence it.

He looked up ahead past the skiing rope and Jožka's bank-heist getaway driver tableau. They were almost back at the *Mandjet*.

As they were arriving, Arun climbed down the ladder to the docking pen, looking anxious. He helped Jožka tie up the runabout, then he jumped into the ocean and swam out to inspect the drone.

"How long do you think it was broadcasting?" he asked Matt. He was treading water, wearing a wrench attached to a cord around his neck.

"Maybe two minutes."

Arun thought it over. "We'll be fine. Even if someone works out exactly what happened, they won't know exactly where."

He got the wrench free and tossed it to Matt. Matt removed the satellite dish, then loosened each of the cores of the rotors. He glanced up at Arun, who was grinning now.

"Can we keep it?" Arun pleaded. "I promise I'll look after it."

"Sorry, this one already has a home."

Matt climbed off into the water; the drone bobbed up but the rotors stayed quiet. He swam away, then followed Arun back to the docking pen and the three of them hauled in the catch.

• • •

Matt said, "I hope they're clear that this thing isn't a weapon." The drone could play recorded warnings, and log video of incursions onto its new owners' land, but if people chose to ignore it, no one could flick a switch and smite their foes from afar.

Eduardo smiled and adjusted the ropes on the tarpaulin. "They're clear, but they don't want everyone to know that. They're going to stick a fake gun on it, and stage something where it looks like it kills a pig."

Matt wasn't sure what to make of that, but if the robotic scarecrow was as much a placebo for the coffee growers as a nocebo for any would-be trespassers, so long as it left people feeling secure enough to join the flotilla he'd be satisfied that it had been worth the risk.

"Are we close?" he asked.

"We're close," Eduardo confirmed.

Matt wanted to ask him about a dozen of their mutual friends from the rigs, but he was afraid to hear the answer, sorting the men into categories: who was coming south, who was aiming for China, who was staying put. He couldn't predict anyone's fate, or change anyone's mind, but the three strategies could not all turn out equally well.

"I'll call you soon," Eduardo said.

"Okay."

Matt clambered over the side of the fishing boat, into the runabout where Arun was waiting.

As they headed back toward the *Mandjet,* Arun said, "Two of my cousins died last week. I just heard the news this morning."

"Jesus. What happened?"

"They were up in Kashmir, trying to make arrangements to take their families there for the summer. The police found their bodies by the side of the road. Their wallets were gone, but the staff from the hotel they were staying in ID'd them."

"I'm sorry."

Arun said, "I keep trying to tell myself that there's a solution for everyone. But how many people can relocate to another city, let alone cross into China?"

"I don't know." Matt struggled to find something positive to say. If there was any way that the rest of Arun's family could have joined the ones who were already in Tasmania, they would have done it by now.

Arun turned to him and declared, almost calmly, "Half the country's going to die in the next few months. Six or seven hundred million people."

Matt wanted to protest, but however vehement his gut response there was nothing he could say to refute the prediction. And Arun didn't seem to expect a reply.

When they entered the docking pen, Matt squinted back across the water. Eduardo's boat had almost vanished from sight. It was still early, but the sun was starting to bite.

"Antarctica, then," Arun said.

"Antarctica," Matt replied.

PART THREE

10

Matt slept late and woke to the sound of the children arriving for school, talking and laughing among themselves as they delivered scraps from their boats into the compost. He walked out onto the deck and gazed down at the ocean; the cheerful yellow "*ônibus escolar*" was heading away from the *Mandjet* to pick up another group. In the distance, a dozen or so members of the flotilla appeared almost motionless, notwithstanding their visible wakes and trailing diesel plumes. It had taken a while for everyone to learn to match each other's pace, but the system they'd hammered out finally seemed to be working, with no stragglers and no impatient vanguard breaking away from the pack.

It was almost seven o'clock. Matt felt like he'd spent the night basting in sweat, but there was no point showering before he'd cleaned up the spillage around the hatch to the compost heap and redistributed the contents within. The kids did their best, but the moldy vegetable peel and fish bones really needed to be stirred in.

"Good morning," Hélia said, walking past on her way

to the shaded stretch of deck where the children were gathering. Matt mumbled something incoherent, embarrassed by his stench and half-nakedness.

He returned to his cabin to wait for the last of the arrivals so he could go and clean up. He sat on his bed, swigging water and checking the news on his phone.

Singapore had recently finished enclosing itself in toughened photovoltaic glass, and was now entirely climate-controlled; the event was being marked with a public holiday, to be known as Thirty Degree Day. Dubai had embarked on a similar plan, but Shanghai was opting for a multitude of smaller domes.

The week's tally for drownings in the Mediterranean had reached four digits, and five in the South China Sea. There were reports of fleets moving south from Somalia, Kenya, Tanzania, Mozambique and Madagascar—but South Africa was already hosting three times its usual population, while struggling with shortages and outbreaks of disease. There'd be no sanctuary there, just crowded camps full of parched, famished people. The only thing those boats could do was keep heading south.

Overnight, the credit-rating agencies had downgraded Australian government debt to junk status, and the Australian dollar had responded with a 60 percent drop in value. Matt tried calling Selena, but the number didn't even ring; the satellite link trilled three ascending tones, then a synthetic voice began chanting a sequence of digits that must have been an error code. He composed a short email; it didn't bounce, but he received no immediate reply.

He heard the class starting, with the children greeting Hélia in unison. He went to deal with the compost, then took a shower, dressed, and headed for the mess, taking the long way around so as not to disrupt the lesson.

By the time he arrived, he was drenched in sweat again. The crew had finished breakfast, but everyone was still sitting around in a stupor, except for Jožka, who was on watch. "Anyone got through to an Australian number lately?" Matt asked.

"I've had no luck all week," Aaron replied.

Arun said, "I've got through to Launceston, but I heard that a lot of the towers on the mainland are out."

"Just from the heat?" Perth had had a run in the low fifties, but if that was unprecedented for the city itself it wasn't much worse than the highest temperatures remote towers in the state's northwest would have faced pre-Taraxippus.

"I think it's a matter of breakdown rates versus the rate of repairs," Arun replied. "Maybe the crews are struggling to keep up—and they might be facing parts shortages."

"Yeah."

In the silence, Matt could hear the class again. "There's

one skill we'll all have for life now," Yuki joked. "Multiplication tables in Portuguese."

"They sound happy," Aaron said. "Don't you think?"

The last reports from Dili had put the temperature in the mid-fifties, even with the constant rain. The children who had come south were doing well, so far, but they were one in a thousand.

· · ·

Matt was on watch in the control room when Eduardo called on the VHF.

"We have visitors," he said. "One boat out of Sri Lanka. They're asking for drinking water. Over."

"Okay. Can you spare it from your own stock, and top up from here later? Over." That seemed simpler than having the Sri Lankan boat try to rendezvous with the *Mandjet*.

"No, they're down to nothing, and they have sixty people on board. They're going to need more than I have here." Eduardo hesitated. "I don't think they're in great shape. Maybe you can ask Rosa if she'll take a look at them? Over."

"Okay. Send them through. Over and out."

Matt stepped out with the binoculars and watched the pale blue vessel approaching. It looked like a small commercial fishing trawler, but even from a distance it was clear that there were people on every square meter of the deck, lying or sitting beneath a patchwork of shade-cloths.

Rosa usually came on board the *Mandjet* with the children from her boat, unless she'd been called to a home visit. Matt found her in the clinic and explained the situation.

"Sixty people?" she muttered. "What were they thinking?" She picked up her bag. "You'd better bring Arun."

Matt was perplexed. "Why? They don't speak Hindi in Sri Lanka."

Rosa stared at him irritably. "I do know that, thank you. And don't take offense, but I'd like a second body-guard before I step onto a boat with that many strangers."

"Okay." Matt went to look for Arun, trying not to dwell on his own clumsiness. He always managed to say the wrong thing to Rosa.

They hauled fifty liters of water to the runabout then went out and met up with the trawler. There was a name written on the side in a rotund script that Matt supposed was Tamil, but in any case was beyond his powers to turn into a string of phonemes. The deck was only three meters or so above the water line, but the sea was rough, and the only way on board was a rope ladder—which seemed to act as a pendulum driven by the waves, refusing to simply hang in place. After some shouted discussions with two of the fishermen, they worked out a way to winch up the containers and Rosa's medical bag, rather than try to carry them on the ladder. Then they ascended with their hands free to help them fend off collisions with the hull, arriving only lightly bruised.

"I'm Suthan," one of the men said. "My friend is Thiru." The boarding party introduced themselves. The fishermen's thick beards almost hid their sunken cheeks, but their T-shirts hung loosely on their shoulders.

"Thank you for the water," Thiru said. "We had nothing." Matt glanced across at the families camped on the deck beneath their makeshift awnings; by now almost everyone had a cup or bottle in their hand. But they all looked half-starved, and he could see at least five babies among them.

"We'll bring some more soon," Arun promised. "But if there's anyone sick here, Rosa's a doctor."

Suthan turned to her and held a palm against his chest. "Thank you, Miss."

While Suthan led Rosa across the deck toward a crying child, Matt surveyed the state of the boat. Structurally, it appeared to be in good shape; ten or twenty people, well supplied, could probably have completed the journey in it—if not in comfort, in reasonable safety.

"How long have you been at sea?" he asked Thiru.

"Five weeks."

"Do you have food?"

"We catch some fish. There's rice . . ." He gestured be-lowdecks. Matt could only assume that they'd been rationing the rice with an iron will, but if they tried to eke it out over the entire summer, from the way they looked now that wasn't going to end well.

Arun said, "We have fresh vegetables." He turned to Matt. "Do you know what's in surplus at the moment?"

"Eggplants," Matt replied. "Probably other things too."

Thiru frowned in puzzlement. "Aubergine?" Arun tried. "*Brinjal? Baingan?*"

Thiru nodded. "*Wambatu.* Maybe we can trade."

"You have dried chilies?" Arun asked.

"Yes." Thiru opened a hatch and motioned to Arun to follow him belowdecks to inspect the goods, but when his feet reached the third or fourth rung of the ladder, Arun changed his mind and ascended. "It must be seventy down there," he said. Thiru returned, dripping with sweat, and offered a small burlap sack to Arun, who inhaled from it cautiously then signaled his approval.

Rosa approached. "I'm going to need to take two adult patients and three children and their mothers back to the *Mandjet.* Nothing infectious, but it's better if they're not in such crowded conditions while they're recovering."

All three mothers proved strong enough to descend

the rope ladder with their children secured in slings on their backs. Matt ferried them across and asked Yuki to show them to the clinic while he loaded some more water and returned. The two sick adults, a man and a woman, were not really ambulatory; after some long discussions, Arun took the woman down the ladder clinging to his back, and then the man was lowered on an improvised stretcher hanging from three ropes, with small teams of people above and below controlling his descent to keep him from striking the side of the trawler.

It was midmorning, and the heat was already unbearable; even the bright, broken reflection off the choppy water felt like a second sun. Matt had done nothing that would normally have taxed him, but as he untied the ropes holding the runabout to the trawler, he felt more spent than he ever had at the end of a twelve-hour shift.

"Bring on the icebergs," Arun pleaded.

Matt winced. "Careful what you wish for."

None of the patients had much English, so Thiru came with them to the *Mandjet* to translate. Matt spent the rest of the morning organizing cabins for the new arrivals; Rosa declared that she'd stay and watch over them for the next few days.

Matt called a crew meeting in the mess and brought everyone up to speed on the encounter. "We can't just give these people food and water and send them on their way," he argued. "Their boat's intact, but it's not safe with that many passengers."

Yuki said, "So what do we do when the next boat's falling apart, but we've already filled up all the cabins?"

"I don't know. We'll work out what's possible at the time." Matt understood the need to reserve some spare capacity for the most urgent situations, but the fact that the trawler wasn't sinking didn't stop it from being a disaster in the making.

"Not wanting to sound callous, but there might be some advantages for us," Jožka suggested. "There are going to be other boats coming down from Sri Lanka. If we're already on good terms with one, that could make it easier to get along with the others. We'll have people to translate, people to vouch for us . . . it could preempt a lot of friction."

Aaron said, "Can't you use an app to translate?"

Jožka snorted. "The aim is *not* to start a war."

Matt looked to Arun. "I'm in favor," Arun said. "Assuming it's up to us."

"What do you mean?"

"There are a thousand other people who might have something to say."

Matt was taken aback. "There was no agreement that they'd get to veto anything the *Mandjet* did. We don't dictate what happens on the other boats."

"Okay." Arun hesitated. "But I still think we should consult on this. Sound it out with Eduardo and let him talk to people, so it doesn't just fall from the sky."

Matt still felt ambivalent. It was hard enough for the four of them to reach consensus; subjecting the *Mandjet* to the communal will of the entire flotilla would be unmanageable. But he called Eduardo and broached the subject.

"Give me a few days to smooth the waters," Eduardo said. "It's the right thing to do, but . . . you know. Better not to bruise any egos."

When Eduardo signed off, Matt tried calling Selena, but he had no more luck than before. If the towers were failing, maybe the landlines were still working. He dialed the front desk at the law firm where she worked.

"The number you have called is not in service," a cheerful inhuman voice explained. Matt checked the company's website; all the details still matched the ones on his phone.

In two days, the *Mandjet* would be due west of Perth. If his family needed to evacuate, that would be the time to do it. Selena had kept reassuring him that everything was fine and they were happy staying put—but that had been before the government went bankrupt and the currency turned to toilet paper.

And if they needed to get out, but still balked at the

Antarctic option? Matt went to the Qantas website and searched for flights from Perth to Hobart. They were booked solid for the next six months, and the other airlines were no different.

Out of curiosity, he checked for flights to Europe. Here, it wasn't a matter of the seats being taken; there were no flights scheduled at all. Nothing to Tokyo, either. Even Yuki and Jožka could not have flown home, notwithstanding their rights as citizens; the political barriers had hardened into something more logistical. He changed the departure site to Cape Town, then Buenos Aires; it made no difference, there was still nothing crossing the equator.

Matt wasn't sure why he was so discomfited by this revelation; when tens of thousands of people were dying every day in border camps, he wasn't going to shed tears for the death of business class. Maybe he'd been clinging to a kind of comforting cynicism, in which the problems of the world still stemmed, in the end, from the same root causes as ever. But if no amount of money and no favored passport could carry you north, then nor would any enlightened rearrangement of those merely human things suffice. Nations could rise and fall, merging or melting away like clouds, but the heat would dictate its own borders.

• • •

It was almost midnight when Selena called. Matt had been drifting in and out of sleep, dragged back toward consciousness every time his dreaming mind found a new, nagging metaphor to alert him to the heat he was trying to ignore. When his ring tone bludgeoned him awake, for a moment he was sure it was just another synesthetic rendition of the prickling of his skin and the suffocating weight of the humid air.

"What's happening?" he rasped. "I thought you were all dead."

He hadn't meant to say anything of the kind, but Selena just took it as hyperbole, or sarcasm. "The phones are playing up here."

"Even at your office?"

The line went silent for a second, but she hadn't been cut off. "The firm closed down last week, but I'd been expecting that for a while. Don't freak out, I still have money in the bank."

"What kind of money in what kind of bank?" Matt had converted his last thousand Australian dollars to a US-dollar PayPal balance a month ago, so at least he'd be able to keep up the payments on the satellite link for a while.

"Just trust me," she replied. "Ninety percent of my job was financial instruments."

"So, not in the Cayman Islands?"

"We're going to be all right," Selena insisted. "We've stockpiled food, the PV is putting out more than we can use and the aircon's still doing its thing."

"What about water?" Matt had checked the dam levels on the web, and they weren't great, but the desalination plant was still operating.

"Nothing in the rainwater tank, obviously, but there's a total ban on garden use, and a twenty-thousand-dollar fine for flushing with anything but gray water or showering for longer than three minutes. That ought to leave us with plenty to drink."

"So your life now is sitting at home with your parents, with the windows closed, going stir-crazy?"

"That's rich, from someone stuck on a boat."

"This boat's going places. You should come and see the penguins, before they all roast."

"No thanks."

Matt said, "What happens if your power supply fails?"

"We're still on good terms with the neighbors. We could stay with them while we wait to get it fixed."

"Even if that takes months?"

Selena groaned. "And what happens if your own machines break down? Do you have an infinite supply of spare parts, for everything?"

"No." And there was no point demanding to know

what she was going to do for food once the freezer was empty, when he couldn't swear that the *Mandjet* would come through the summer with its fish stocks and garden intact.

He said, "Just promise me—"

The connection cut out. Matt tried calling back, redialing the number every five minutes for more than an hour, but all he got was the same error message.

• • •

Eduardo came back with an answer: the powers that be were prepared to invite the Sri Lankans into the flotilla. "Maybe you can talk to them informally, first, just to see if they actually want to join us. If they do, I'll bring the old men there and we can make it official."

Matt found Thiru in the clinic and took him aside. "We've talked it over, and we're hoping your group will stay with us for the rest of the journey."

Thiru looked puzzled. "Why?"

Matt said, "Hundreds of boats will be coming from Sri Lanka. What if we need to trade with them, or form some kind of alliance? If we don't have any Tamil or Sinhala speakers among us, all of that could be much harder."

Thiru considered this. "Let me talk to my friends."

The next morning, a dozen Timorese and a dozen Sri

Lankans squeezed into the mess, with Eduardo and Suthan translating and the crew of the *Mandjet* looking on. Matt listened to the speeches, as florid as those of any diplomatic summit, but he wasn't in the mood to be cynical, and he believed both parties were sincere.

Jožka turned to him and whispered, "Welcome to the Republic of the South."

"Can we build our capital at the pole?"

"Maybe just the Summer Palace."

Matt smiled. Republic or not, here they were: all eleven hundred of them, still afloat. And beside them in the distance, who knew how many thousands of boats.

But however vast the fleet, however crowded the decks and holds of every fleeing vessel, they would always be outnumbered by the ones they'd left behind.

11

Matt could judge the height of the waves without leaving his bunk, or even opening his eyes. As his segment of the *Mandjet* seesawed between its pivots, tilting the cabin and agitating some spirit level in his inner ear, the whole geometry of the structure played out in his mind's eye, a ship in a bottle come to life inside his skull. All he had to do was compare the waves he saw with the scale of the pontoons that were riding them, to arrive at the result: *seven meters.*

He opened his eyes. It was almost dawn. There'd be no school again today for the Timorese; it wasn't worth the risk of someone getting hurt moving from vessel to vessel. But Hélia had been giving classes in English to the ten Sri Lankan children permanently on board, and she'd moved into a cabin of her own so she wouldn't have to keep making the crossing.

Matt got up and took a shower. For the first time in a long while, the seawater felt cool on his skin, and when he turned off the flow and stood in the wind it dried him in seconds by sheer force, not heat. He was starting to believe that latitude alone really could save their lives.

There were low clouds in the east, turning the sunrise red over the gray ocean. He could see two unfamiliar boats in the distance among the flotilla, so he went to join Jožka in the control room.

"Do we know who they are?" he asked.

"Indonesians," she replied. "They talked on the radio with Martinho's boat; they're not wanting to trade anything, they're just passing through."

"Okay." Matt was never sure if he was over-sensitive to Indonesian-Timorese tensions; there'd been a couple of Sumatran workers on the rigs, and they'd got on well enough with all of their colleagues. But it was hard to imagine Martinho effusively welcoming a boatload of his former enemies into the flotilla.

Matt made his way to the mess, keeping one hand cupped around the safety rail so he could grab it in an instant if the slant of the deck threatened his footing. The mess was already packed with boisterous children and their parents, but when he hung back at the doorway some of the kids came and dragged him in, tugging at his hands and bombarding him with questions.

"Why did you make your ship like a circle?" Sundara asked.

"To hold the fish in the middle."

"Why don't they just swim away underneath?"

"There's a net underneath."

"So why do you need the ship around them? Why not just the net?"

"That would work, too," Matt conceded. "But this way, there's more room for people. And it's easier to get electricity from the waves."

Thiru approached and spoke in Tamil to his nephew, who turned to Matt. "Am I pestering you, sir?"

"No, it's all right."

Thiru led Matt over to his table and gestured to him to share the food already laid out.

"We have bananas?" Matt couldn't process this. "Who did we get bananas from?"

"Madagascans," Thiru replied matter-of-factly. "They had too many of them. We gave them potatoes in exchange."

This was the first Matt had heard of that encounter. "How long will they last?"

Thiru pointed to some fried ones on another plate. "Those were a bit . . ." He rocked his hand. "But the rest we can make into flour."

"Okay." Matt clung to his seat as the floor tipped and some of the plates threatened to slide out of the indentations molded into the table. *Ten meters.*

His phone rang in his pocket; it was Jožka.

"The *Sophia*'s asking for help," she said. "Can you handle it? Eduardo's already working on another ship."

"All right, tell them I'll be out there in fifteen minutes."

Matt excused himself and went to fetch his tools. As the deck rocked beneath him, he could hear the pontoons creaking from the stress. *How many cycles of this much flexure was the fiberglass rated for?* He was sure it had added up to decades when he'd first sat down to work on the design, but none of the actual numbers were coming back to him.

In the runabout, the wind brought the spray in like a rainstorm on a roller coaster, and the sight of each approaching crest towering over him summoned up a visceral dread that nothing he'd endured in the past could really neutralize. He had never been in a vessel so mismatched with the ocean around it. He slapped his chest to remind himself that he hadn't forgotten his life jacket.

When he reached the *Sophia,* Luís threw a rope down, but when Matt had secured his end he found the runabout bashing itself against the side of the larger boat, with enough violence to do damage.

Luís shouted, "We need to bring it up on deck!"

He threw down two more ropes, and Matt attached them to the bow and stern. Then he put on the backpack with his tools and climbed the middle rope the short distance to the deck. Luís called a friend over to help, and the three of them winched the runabout up from the water.

Matt's legs were trembling. "Well, that was fun."

Luís led Matt down to the engine room, where his hopes to have escaped the heat proved premature.

"Do you want to start it up?" Matt asked.

Luís obliged. Matt listened carefully to the shuddering sound, gingerly placing a hand on the driveshaft casing.

"It's not the engine or the driveshaft," he declared glumly. "It's the propeller."

Luís didn't seem surprised; he'd probably just been seeking a second opinion. "So what can we do?"

Matt was close to gagging from the diesel fumes, so he took a few steps toward the ladder and Luís got the hint and accompanied him up onto the deck.

Back in Timor, the *Sophia* could have limped home, under sail or towed by another boat, to be dragged onto the beach for repairs. But they were almost a thousand kilometers from land. None of the vessels could tow it all the way to Antarctica without the pair falling far behind the rest of the flotilla.

Matt watched the kids burning off energy, chasing each other back and forth across the wildly tilting deck, shrieking with laughter every time they almost lost their balance. There were thirty people on the *Sophia*; if they all came onto the *Mandjet* it would be painfully crowded, but maybe they could be split up among the other boats.

And the next time? And the next? Until half the boats

in the flotilla were as packed as Thiru's trawler had been?

He turned to Luís. "There is one thing I could try. I've trained for it, but it was in calmer waters, with a stationary target."

Luís didn't catch his meaning straight away, and Matt felt his courage deserting him. Maybe one of the other ex-Sunrise workers in the flotilla had done the same course. Matt scoured his brain for the faces of his fellow students, before they'd donned their helmets. Nuno had been there . . . but he'd taken his family north. Álvaro had been there . . . but Matt had no idea where he was now.

"Ah!" Luís smiled. "You learned the underwater welding!"

. . .

Jožka put out a call to the whole flotilla to cut their engines, so the *Sophia* wouldn't fall behind. Matt asked Arun to check the welding gear, to make sure the insulation was in good shape.

"When you were doing this before, did you get a metallic taste in your mouth?" Arun inquired, peering at his multimeter as he probed the electrode holder.

"I did," Matt replied. "The instructor told us it could decompose our fillings, eventually. But I never planned on making a career of it."

"They didn't tell you the trick to avoid that?"

"What trick? Isn't the seawater ionized...?" Matt trailed off; he had no idea how that could make his saliva more acidic, given that he wouldn't actually be gargling the ocean.

Arun smiled. "The water's got nothing to do with it. Just don't let the power cable wrap across the back of your neck. Some divers do that to control it without using their hands, but when it's that close, it can induce currents in your dental amalgam."

"Okay." Matt had more pressing worries than the state of his fillings, but a toothache in Antarctica would be worth avoiding. "So am I going to get electrocuted, or not?"

"Not if you're careful. How are you going to keep yourself in place?"

"Good question."

Matt didn't have what he needed on the *Mandjet,* so he scrounged spare pieces of timber from across the flotilla. The frame would attach to the stern of the *Sophia,* reaching back under the hull to one side of the rudder to provide a fixed platform an arm's length from the propeller. The ship didn't come with a blueprint or a CAD file, but it was possible to infer most of the dimensions just by pacing things out, and when Luís surfaced after a round of preliminary repairs to pave the way for the welding, he was able to fill in the remaining details.

By the time Matt was done it was late in the afternoon. He started up the air pump, put on his helmet and climbed down the frame into the water, trailing the same hose and cables he'd need when he did the job for real, but leaving the power supply disconnected.

The hull dipped and rose with every passing wave, but its inertia and rigidity kept it from going with the flow entirely, and the residual tug of the water was more than enough to threaten to tear him loose. He held the frame tightly as he made his way around the turn, wondering if the whole plan was going to end up like brain surgery in a dodgem car, but by the time he reached the end—a little more sheltered, and a little closer to the center of the ship—the forces trying to dislodge him were beginning to seem almost manageable.

Luís had already spent an hour in a web of ropes he'd slung between the rudder and the driveshaft, hammering out the dent in the propeller blade, more or less restoring its shape. All that remained was to weld the torn edges together.

Matt inspected the surface; the metal was clean. He strapped himself to the chair at the end of the frame and checked his reach and stability, then he spoke into the intercom.

"Can you hear me up there?"

Luís replied, "I hear you."

"Have you ever seen damage like this?"

"Only in the shallow water. Hitting a reef, hitting rocks."

"You seen any ice around?" Matt asked.

Luís laughed. "Not yet."

Matt hadn't meant it as a joke. The water they were in was far from freezing, but all the extra sea ice that had formed over the new, deeper winter wouldn't vanish overnight, and it might travel hundreds of kilometers north before it melted away completely.

The hull began to execute a new kind of violent gyration; the waves weren't just higher, there had to be a crosswind making them choppy.

Luís said, "The weather's getting crazy. Finish it tomorrow."

"Yeah, I'm coming up."

Luís invited Matt to stay on the *Sophia* overnight, sharing a meal with his family, sleeping on the deck beside his cousins. Matt gazed up at the stars for a while, but there was nothing restful about the way they traced Lissajous curves across his field of vision.

"Your family's in Australia?" Jorge whispered to Matt from his blanket a meter or so away. Matt supposed he was in his late teens; he looked younger, but he never came to school.

"Yeah."

"How come you didn't bring them with you?"

"They thought they'd be safer where they are."

Jorge said, "I wanted my friends to come on the *Sophia*. But their parents wanted to stay in Timor-Leste." His voice thickened as he spoke the last few words; Matt glanced over and saw his face contorted.

Matt said, "Maybe they got out and went north."

"I don't think so."

As far as Matt knew, no one in the flotilla had heard any news out of Dili for a week, but across the region people had been succumbing to the heat. Once the humidity was high enough to render perspiration ineffective, once shifting blood flow to the skin started damaging other organs and causing more harm than good, there was nothing the body could do to protect itself. Without air-conditioning, you were dead. The sick, the elderly, the children first, but in the end, everyone who couldn't escape or conjure up some mechanical aid.

"I know the grid's hopeless in Dili," Matt conceded, "but there are a lot of small generators." It was no use invoking solar power when there was torrential rain. "And people will look out for each other, won't they?"

"They'll try," Jorge replied. But he sounded no more reassured than he would have been by the idea of solidarity in Hell.

Matt glanced up at the sky again; the view was no less

dizzying than before, but it seemed apt now. Everything was deranged, and it made no sense to seek tranquility.

• • •

An hour or so after dawn, Matt decided that the sea was unlikely to grow calmer. Luís joined him at the stern; they tested the intercom, then went through the protocol together.

Matt said, "If I stop answering, shut off the power, pull out the leads, and come and get me."

"Okay." Luís paused, then shook his head. "No, this isn't right. I'm going to bring Rosa here."

"You don't have to do that."

"You want to be resuscitated by me, or her?" Luís grinned. "I know she's scary, but swallow your pride."

He went to make a call on the radio. Matt sat on the deck, his hands shaking. There was no one else in sight; though only the driveshaft would be electrified, everyone on the boat had already been corralled into places where they couldn't accidentally touch any metal part that might end up live if things went awry.

Twenty minutes later, Rosa arrived, clambering up from the runabout Yuki had driven from the *Mandjet*. She spoke to Luís and went belowdecks. "She's going to check on the kids, but she's there if we need her," Luís explained.

"Okay."

Luís started up the air pump. Matt put on his helmet and turned toward the water. Leaning over the stern as it rose up on a crest, he stared down into the approaching foam-flecked valley and tried to synchronize his expectations with the impending flows and forces. If he could take the whole *Mandjet* into his skull, this ought to be no harder.

He climbed onto the frame and began to descend, but he'd barely placed a toe in the water when the stern dropped and the hull rose up in front of him, tipping him backward. He clung on tightly and waited for the angles to reverse; if he lost his hold and ended up adrift, he'd feel like some kind of half-drowned rodeo clown trying to scramble back into the saddle, and he could easily break a limb in the process.

Once he was immersed he made his way quickly along the frame and strapped himself into the chair. He'd remembered to turn in the right direction, so the hose and cables hadn't ended up tangled. "Can you hear me?" he asked Luís.

"Loud and clear."

"I'm just getting organized."

"No rush."

Matt switched on the lamp at the side of his helmet and reached up toward the damaged propeller, getting a feel for the disposition of his joints and muscles that he'd need to maintain throughout the weld. He shifted in the chair, trying to find the most comfortable posture to work from, and when the water dragged him askew he forced himself back into place and tightened the straps.

He unclipped the electrode holder from his belt and reached out again toward the propeller. Even with a gloved hand, the sight of the bare electrode protruding just centimeters above his grip was unsettling. The current would flow from the power supply on deck through the cable that snaked down to the engine room, along the drive shaft into the propeller, then jump the arc to the electrode and return through the cable that Matt had dutifully kept from curling around the back of his neck. So long as that circuit remained available, the flow of charge had no reason to enter his body. He'd done this before and survived; he wasn't going to start regressing to some superstitious vision of electric power as a malicious force that would reach out through the seawater, spurning the path of least resistance, like a leopard abandoning a perfectly delicious dead gazelle to pursue him if he dared to catch its eye.

Matt forced himself to breathe slowly, then spent a minute checking that he really did know which way the water would be tugging on him, second by second. The real danger would come if he lost control of the electrode and grabbed it in the wrong place before he had time to think.

He lowered the visor over his helmet then turned the lamp up to full strength; the beam was powerful enough to let him see the propeller through the protective shield. He moved the tip of the electrode into place, just above the start of the break in the metal.

"Power on," he said.

The arc lit up and the water all but vanished, bleached into crystalline transparency. In the periphery of his vision, he saw the unstoppable flow dragging bubbles and swirling debris through the stark radiance, but he shut out the light show and focused on the tiny, tamed sun that was oozing liquid metal into the propeller's wound.

He traced the torn edge slowly. It was impossible to see what was happening at the point of the arc itself, but the fresh surface it was leaving behind looked smooth and clean and whole. The electrode holder was warm from the current; Matt could feel it through his glove. But unless the waves tossed the *Sophia* so high that the propeller came out of the water, the ocean would keep carrying the heat away.

After a few minutes, his forearm began to cramp. "Power off," he said, and the arc vanished.

"Everything okay?"

"Yeah."

Matt rubbed his arm and inspected the propeller. He was about one-sixth of the way down the first edge, and so far he hadn't screwed up.

He shifted the electrode holder to his left hand and waggled his arm, then let it hang in the water, tugged at by the flow as the stern descended. If he kept his focus, and kept a steady hand, he could do this twelve more times.

· · ·

When Luís started up the engine, Matt stood beside him in silence, straining his ears. There weren't going to be any X-rays of these welds, or neutron diffraction analyses to grade them. The repair would hold good until it didn't, a success until it failed.

After a few minutes with nothing but the ordinary throb and hiss of the engine, Luís's tentative smile broadened. He turned to Matt and shook his hand. "Good job."

"You too."

"Let's hope it's the last time."

Matt said, "Just keep a lookout for the ice."

Yuki came and picked up Matt and Rosa, then dropped Rosa off at her own boat. The waves were no tamer than the day before, but Matt found them less daunting, having survived a prolonged dunking with live wires.

Yuki was quiet as they approached the *Mandjet*. "How are things with your family?" Matt asked.

"They're fine," she replied. "My mother's teaching Japanese to Filipino refugees. She said it makes her feel more useful than any of the jobs she did before."

"That's good." Matt waited, resisting an urge to fill the silence.

"To be honest," Yuki added, "I wish I was there with her. When we first headed north to get out of the cold, I thought we'd keep going: we'd carry a few passengers up to Siberia, and I could get off on the way back. But then the plan turned out differently. I should have left when we were in Darwin, but I felt bad at the thought of walking out on everyone."

"There might be flights again, in autumn," Matt suggested.

"From where?"

"Perth."

Yuki laughed. "You really think Perth will have a functioning airport three months from now?"

Matt didn't know what he believed. "Hobart, then. Or Christchurch. The current's taking us east anyway. Maybe we'll loop back to Dili along the Pacific route."

"Maybe." Yuki made it sound as if he might as well have been discussing Santa's delivery plans.

"So will you take Aaron to Japan with you?" Matt

asked. "I guess you could apply for some kind of spouse visa—?"

Yuki turned to him with an expression of incredulity. He said, "Okay, so we'll find a way to get him to his parents in Cobar."

They reached the *Mandjet* and spent fifteen minutes trying to get the runabout tied up, while the waves seemed intent on ejecting it from the docking pen. Matt went to his cabin and sat on his bunk, then picked up his phone to check for news from Perth.

Lightning had started a fire overnight, in the hills that wrapped the eastern rim of the city. It had spread west rapidly, incinerating bushland and thousands of homes. The news sites were all showing the same satellite image, with charred, smoke-shrouded ground all the way to Midland, a few kilometers from his parents' house.

Matt tried contacting Selena by every method he could think of, but all he got was a new set of error messages. He switched back to the news. There didn't seem to be any professional journalists covering the fire on the ground, but the sites had pulled clips off the social media of a handful of people with satellite phones. The scenes were all flames and chaos; there were no images of evacuees being tended to in air-conditioned safety. On Twitter, almost everything tagged #PerthFire was a plea from an anxious relative elsewhere for someone in the fire zone to get in touch.

He sat pawing at the screen, trying to find some magic combination of taps and swipes that would make the problem tractable. Then he snapped out of the trance and rose to his feet. He stuffed two pairs of shoes and a wide-brimmed hat into his backpack, then headed for the workshop.

He chose a three-kilowatt-hour battery, the largest he could carry unaided, a photovoltaic panel about half a meter on each side, and the leads he'd need to make everything work. Then he lugged it all to the mess and filled a ten-liter bottle with water. The families were eating lunch; Matt felt the children's hands snatch at his wrists, but he was deaf to whatever they were saying.

On his way to the runabout, he saw Jožka approaching in the opposite direction.

"Do you need a hand?" Jožka asked, eyeing his unwieldy baggage.

"No thanks."

"Where are you off to?"

"Home."

"What?"

Matt brushed past her.

"What's happening? Matt?" She caught up with him. "Are you going to tell me what's going on?"

"There's been a fire," he replied brusquely, wishing he

could outpace her, but it was all that he could do to keep his balance. "The whole city's falling apart. I need to bring them here."

"All right." Jožka edged ahead of him. "So how are you planning on getting there?"

"I'm taking one of the runabouts."

"Okay." She glanced away, and seemed to make eye contact with someone behind them, but Matt was too weighed down to follow her gaze. She said, "Do you really think it will go the distance?"

"I can keep charging it. I've got everything I need."

"I'm not talking about power, I'm talking about the waves."

Matt said, "I just came here through the waves. Ask Yuki."

"You came a few hundred meters. That's not the same thing."

"Yes it is. You just repeat it and repeat it."

Jožka looked back again, then Arun and Thiru appeared in some kind of flanking maneuver.

"Matt, talk to me," Arun pleaded. "We can work something out. If you do it like this, you're either going to drown before you get there, or the four of you will drown coming back."

"Work what out?" Matt retorted. "Do you think the whole flotilla is going to turn around and sail into the heat, just so I can look for my family?" Even if he'd asked for the *Mandjet* alone, that would have meant killing all the cobia.

Thiru said, "No, brother, but we can go in my boat."

"What?"

"It's the best choice," Thiru insisted. "There's only ten people left on board. I can bring them here in half an hour, then we'll go. What do you say?"

Matt stopped walking. "Is this a trick?" If it was, Arun didn't seem to have been in on it; he looked as shocked as Matt was.

Thiru shook his head solemnly. "I'm not playing with you. All my family's here, but it was hard to convince them. I know your situation."

The deck lurched, and Matt staggered. He almost lost his grip on the battery, but Jožka reached over and steadied it, taking half the weight as they eased it down together.

Thiru said, "We do this the right way. Not in the small boat, that's crazy."

12

The trawler wasn't slow, but it had to fight the current. Matt sat in the wheelhouse watching Thiru at the helm, steering by hand with his eyes flicking from compass to water, compensating for every sideways shove the endless rows of waves delivered.

"Could be two days," Thiru predicted.

"Yeah." Matt had not been expecting a shorter journey, but he didn't want to dwell on the question of exactly what conditions on the ground could be endured for that long. "Do you ever hear from your village?" he asked.

Thiru shook his head. "If they stayed, they'll be dead. I took everyone who'd come with me."

Matt balked at the finality of this verdict. "Wasn't there some kind of cold storage place, for the fish?"

Thiru glanced at him irritably. "Yes, and it broke down two times a week. Maybe twenty people could stay alive in there—if they have enough supplies and a top-notch mechanic." He added, "I tried to buy AC for my parents' house. By then you couldn't get it at any price. I had a good business, export quality. I always thought by this time I'd make my parents comfortable." He turned to Matt again. "Why'd you build that thing? Did you know what was coming?"

"Not when I started. It was just meant to be a fish farm."

Thiru said, "Some people think the Chinese government knew, ten years ago."

"I doubt that," Matt replied. "You know the glass walls they're building around the big cities in southern China?"

"Yes."

"Do you think they would have let the glass factories waste their time making phone screens for ten years, when they could have got a head start on that project instead?"

Thiru laughed. "Fair point." Something ahead of them caught his eye. "What's that?"

Matt rose to his feet and approached the helm. A jagged white object a couple of meters across was bobbing in the water, barely rising above the surface but refusing to sink or break up as the waves crashed over it. "I think it's ice."

Thiru nodded, smiling slightly. "We should grab it?"

"It might break your net."

"I can fix the net." He seemed as amused as if Matt had expressed a fear that they might get their hands dirty or their feet wet.

"What can your winch pull?"

Thiru took that question more seriously. "It rated fifty tons when it was new, but I'd only trust it for half that."

Matt guessed the miniature iceberg was protruding some thirty centimeters out of the water, which would make it three meters tall, and maybe twelve cubic meters in volume. "This could be eleven tons." The trawler would have taken heavier catches than that, and though the weight would never have been so concentrated, the fish must have been packed with ice for the journey back, even if the blocks were smaller. "You think the floor of your hold is strong enough? If we lay it on its side, that's two tons per square meter."

Thiru thought for a while, maybe doing some mental calculation comparing the loading with past catches. "We can do it," he decided.

When they drew closer, Thiru had Matt take the wheel then went out to cast the net. The iceberg was no longer in sight at all from where Matt stood; he relied on Thiru shouting instructions to keep the boat beside it. It was easy now to imagine how the *Sophia* had been damaged without anyone spotting the danger.

Matt heard the net going in, and then a minute or so later the winch started groaning. He turned to see the dripping iceberg rise up from the water, shaped like a giant's broken tooth. Thiru set the derrick turning and brought the prize around over the hold, then he started lowering it. The boat shuddered as the ice came to rest on the floor, but there was no ominous creaking to suggest that the structure was about to give way.

Thiru dropped the net in and closed the hatch, then returned to the helm and took the wheel.

"Now we have fucking AC," he said.

• • •

The next morning the heat was brutal. They'd come as far west as they needed to and were heading due north, nudging the sun a little higher with every kilometer they traversed. Thiru had been up all night, and he agreed to go and sleep in the hold for a while and let Matt take the wheel.

Matt hadn't expected to sleep much himself, but though he'd felt himself shudder and twitch in his dreams, he'd barely woken. Now that he was traveling in the right direction, the panic he'd felt on the *Mandjet* had subsided. He trusted Selena; if it was humanly possible for the three of them to get out of harm's way, she would have made it happen. And even if a tenth of the city was in flames, even if the grid was down everywhere, there'd still be hundreds of thousands of houses with air conditioners and power of their own.

The wind had fallen away, leaving a steady corrugation of three-meter waves rolling in from the west. Small ships passed by in the distance, alone or in flotillas, heading south. Overhead, the sky was a desert: no clouds, no birds, no aircraft. Matt swigged water dutifully as he steered, two mouthfuls every five minutes by the clock on the helm. As soon as he swallowed, an equivalent quantity of moisture oozed from his skin and ran down his body, but in the still, humid air he could only feel it through its flow; its temperature was no different from his own. Sometimes he felt compelled to look down and reassure himself that the fluid dripping from his calves, every bit as warm as the blood in his veins, really was transparent.

Around noon, Thiru appeared, and Matt retreated to the hold, which stank like a decade's worth of shrimp but was gloriously cool. Once the hatch was closed it was too dark to see anything; the steady drip from the melting iceberg started out distracting but soon turned soporific.

When he woke he climbed out to find that it was evening, but the heat had barely abated. The open sky made the closeness of the air more shocking; how was it possible to swelter without a blanket of clouds, when the space between the stars was just a few degrees from absolute zero?

He greeted Thiru. "I'll take over, if you want a rest," he offered.

"First I'll cook."

Matt hadn't eaten all day, and the thought of food made him queasy, but when Thiru returned with some kind of vegetable pilau his nausea vanished and he joined in gratefully.

"How far is your home from the coast?" Thiru asked.

"A long way," Matt replied, "but not far from the river." He was about to promise that the water levels would pose no threat of the trawler's hull scraping the riverbed, but he was no longer sure that that was true. "If we get there by sunset tomorrow, I'll aim to be back by dawn. If I'm not, you should leave without me." If he hadn't found his family by then, he'd have to take shelter during the daylight hours anyway, and he couldn't ask Thiru to hang around indefinitely while his sole protection from the heat dripped away.

"What happens if you stay?" Thiru asked.

"I'll keep looking, then try to find another boat we can leave on." Matt doubted that Selena would have enough money left to buy them a place, but maybe his experience on the water would carry some weight. "Catch up with the *Mandjet,* if possible."

Thiru nodded, then took the empty plates away. Matt heard him bustling about for a while, then go down into the hold.

He stood at the helm, trying to stay alert by guessing

the next star to rise in the north; he'd thought he knew the constellations well enough, but picturing the way the horizon swept over them to reveal the hidden portions wasn't easy.

There were lights on the water, far away, always receding in the end. Near midnight, a half-moon appeared in the east, but the angle of the waves kept it aloof, and it left no silver trail across the ocean.

· · ·

It was midafternoon when Matt saw the yacht approaching, and he managed to raise it on the VHF. The respondent identified herself as Veronica and her ship as the *Blue Dahlia*.

"I'm heading for Perth," Matt explained. "Do you know the situation there? Over."

"Sorry, no," Veronica replied. "We're coming from Bunbury. The grid's out there, and the batteries are failing. Over."

"Why are the batteries failing? Over."

"From the heat. People have been trying to move them indoors to keep them cool, but you need the right skills. Our neighbors ended up wrecking their system—and we were on the grid ourselves, so we'd been staying with them. The whole place is going to shit. We're trying for

New Zealand. Over."

Matt doubted things were much better there, least of all for new arrivals, but he wasn't going to start second-guessing other people's choices. "Good luck. Over and out."

As the *Blue Dahlia* passed to the west, it came close enough for Matt to see the empty deck gleaming in the sun; most of the passengers would be below in air-conditioned cabins. He felt a twinge, not so much of jealousy, as remorse; if he'd built some kind of luxury yacht instead of the *Mandjet,* maybe his family would have been lured to safety on it months ago.

Thiru rose and joined him at the helm. Matt doubted he could get any sleep himself, now that they were so close to their destination, but Thiru persuaded him to go and cool off for a few hours anyway. The iceberg had lost about a quarter of its volume, and Matt spent ten minutes pumping out the pool of tepid water it had left on the floor of the hold, worried that it might be accelerating the melting.

When he came back on deck it was growing dark, and the GPS put them a couple of kilometers from the mouth of the river. Matt could see no lights from the shore, where the port's gantries were usually studded with flashing beacons. In the distance a curtain of black smoke filled the eastern sky, stretching halfway to the zenith.

An orange glow reached up into the pall; the fire was somewhere over the horizon, but still powerful enough to make itself seen.

They sailed into the inner harbor. A handful of navigation lights remained active, blinking at the water's edge, but behind them all the loading bays and warehouses were blacked out completely. Matt could see the outlines of cranes, shipping containers and trucks in the starlight, but nothing was moving, and there was not so much as a lit cigarette glowing above the silent concrete and asphalt. They took the bend slowly; the trawler's own lights were on high, but they only reached so far into the gloom.

Once they cleared the port, there were patches of intermittent brightness in the distance: a few shops or houses still with power, glimpsed between the dark buildings in the foreground. All Matt could make out on the streets near the riverbank were the silhouettes of cars, parked or abandoned. Far away, a group of people were shouting. The tone was angry and urgent, but none of the words were clear.

Something caught his eye, bobbing along in the expanse of water lit up by the trawler. It resolved into a pale-skinned, blue-tinged corpse, facedown, arms flopping gently. The shirtless back bore an elaborate tattoo, words in some Gothic script now too wrinkled to decipher. Matt thought of asking Thiru to help him retrieve the body so they could deliver it to the appropriate authorities, if any still existed. But if they took on that task, they might never be done with it.

Farther north, peering into the wealthy riverside suburbs, Matt saw more oases of light—a sign of better batteries, or more robust components, or perhaps just the resources to ensure that whatever the system, it was kept cool. He and Arun had spent three days at the start of winter reinstalling his parents' power wall indoors, and even Arun had teased him for his zealousness. But now the whole thing was probably lost to the flames.

A few people had gathered on Pelican Point. They were quiet and still, and it was too dark to get any sense of their demeanor, but they were healthy enough to stand upright. Maybe they'd wandered out of their homes at sunset in the hope of catching a breeze off the water. Maybe they'd found a way to get through the daylight hours without electricity, retreating to underground bunkers with caches of hoarded ice packed in Styrofoam.

"Drink," Thiru urged him.

"Yeah." Matt took a swig from his water bottle; he'd let himself grow parched.

They sailed on, toward the center of the city. On the eastern shore a handful of cars sped down the Kwinana Freeway; it looked like the traffic at three in the morning, not eight at night. As they approached the Causeway, Matt saw a group of people crossing on foot. A woman leaned over the rails and called down to them, "Got a light?"

On the western skyline, near the top of a single office building among a dozen dark companions, random portions of five successive stories were illuminated, as if an attempt to spell out some pixelated public service message with a grid of bright windows had succumbed to a computer crash. Matt saw more people on the riverbank, some wading in the shallows. The water around the trawler was a putrid green now, and stank of something that had bloomed and died.

"Show me all the jetties," Thiru said. "I can see a few, but maybe I'm missing some."

"We still have a way to go."

"I know, but if you don't find your family close to where I leave you, you'll come back this way looking for them, right? If I sail in the morning without you, I can check all the jetties along the way."

"Okay." Matt was ashamed that he hadn't thought of the plan himself. As he pointed to an inconspicuous wooden protrusion near a small playground, he said, "Would you recognize me from this distance, if I was standing there at dawn?"

"I can come closer."

Matt said nothing, but maybe Thiru thought better of

tempting fate. He opened a cabinet under the map table and took out a bundle of folded cloth.

"Hang this from the jetty, and I'll know it's you."

Matt unfolded it enough to see what it was, then stuffed it in his backpack. "Either that, or a stranded Sri Lankan cricket fan."

Thiru laughed. "I hope not. He might want to talk for the whole journey, and cricket is a very boring game."

. . .

As they approached the Garratt Road Bridge, the diffuse orange glow in the northeast acquired a brighter layer of actual flames. Matt couldn't see down to their base to discover exactly what was burning, but considering his location it seemed likely that the source was most of Guildford. The parkland that wound through the suburb would hardly have been lush with new growth after the punishing winter, but if the heat had been enough to dry out every dead tree to its core, then even without an abundance of leaf litter there would have been plenty of fuel.

"That's where they lived," he told Thiru, gesturing toward the conflagration.

"So they would have left for safety. You know where? Some relatives, some friends?"

"I have a cousin. A long way away, though, and maybe his own house wasn't in good shape." Matt couldn't read their minds. All he could do was try to retrace their journey, and hope he picked up some clue along the way.

There was a jetty just past the bridge, on the northern bank of the river. Thiru brought the trawler close enough for Matt to jump down onto the creaking boards.

"See you in the morning, maybe," Matt called back to him. Thiru raised a hand and Matt turned away.

The jetty abutted a concrete path that led to a rowing club. Matt skirted the building and crossed the empty car park. The daytime heat baked into the asphalt was still palpable, and wads of softened tar stuck to the soles of his shoes like discarded chewing gum.

Once he was on a public street he quickly got off the blacktop onto the sandy verge. As he strode north, he passed a small forest of skeletal trees to his left, in what must once have been a park. The houses around him were dark and silent; he could hear no traffic nearby, or insects. But the darkness seemed to breathe and hum, with a spectrum of buzzes and susurrations that felt close, but impossible to localize. Matt took out his water bottle and drank; as he swallowed, all of the phantom sounds vanished.

It could not have been more than a kilometer from the riverbank to the street's fourth intersection—where it met his target, Guildford Road—but he arrived as short of breath as if he'd charged straight up a steep hill. He took another mouthful of water and felt the sweat dribble uselessly down his limbs and torso. He was no longer sure that it had been wise to sleep in the hold beside the ice; it might have spared him some of the cumulative effects of heat stress, but it had also robbed him of the chance to acclimate. For a moment he felt light-headed, as if that imaginary hill had been somewhere in the Andes and he was about to succumb to altitude sickness, but it passed.

He set off westward. This was the route Selena and his parents would have started out on, whatever their ultimate destination. He turned and glanced back toward the fire; amid the flames, he could see glowing embers juggled by the updraft. If there were water trucks trying to hold back the front, they'd either be spread so thin that they'd have no effect at all, or concentrated on saving a handful of chosen areas, elsewhere. The air was mercifully still, and maybe the fire had encountered a couple of northbound roads blocking its way, but it wouldn't take much of a wind to carry its seeds across four lanes.

Ahead of him the roadside was strewn with cars, but he could see nothing moving, and no break in the darkness. No one would have willingly lingered this close to the fire, and he would have hoped that either Selena's car or his parents' was working when they had to flee, but on all the evidence neither old-style nor electric had been coping well with the conditions, and fuel had probably been in short supply for weeks. Even if they'd wanted to reach Leo's house, or some other distant sanctuary, they might have had to settle for something closer.

A few blocks along, he saw a large, silver-furred dog lying stretched out on the road. He lowered his eyes, but then raised them again as he unpicked the afterimage; there was a girl, or a short, slight-framed woman nestled against the animal's belly. Matt approached, refusing to be deterred by the stench in case it had only one source, but once he was closer it was apparent that both had been dead for a while. The girl still held the dog's leash; a metal disk on its collar with cursive engraving caught the starlight. He took out his phone and checked for a signal, but the towers hadn't magically sprung back to life. He squatted down to photograph the tag in close-up; even if the phone number never worked again, the police might be able to use it to trace the girl's family. When the flash went off, he tried to stay focused on the screen, but everything the burst of light revealed in the periphery stamped itself into his brain.

He kept walking, crossing back and forth to make a closer inspection of any car that might have been his family's. The feeble lighting robbed him of most of the depth cues he was used to, undermining his sense of the shape of each vehicle almost as much as it flattened out the difference between paint jobs. All he could do was err on the side of thoroughness, and hope that the shadows couldn't camouflage the thing he sought so perfectly that he'd walk right past it.

When he looked back at the fire the flames appeared more vigorous. He tried walking faster, telling himself it didn't matter if his limbs and lungs felt as strained as if he were sprinting; he wasn't old or sick, he could run for hours if he needed to. In front of him, the stars blazed above the dark buildings, as fierce as they had ever been at sea.

He lost count of the intersections he passed, and it was impossible to make out the street signs, but as he approached the second set of dead traffic lights he smelled the river nearby and thought he knew more or less how far he'd come. As he turned to see if he could glimpse the water, instead he saw a muted hint of artificial light, coming from a building a few stories high, off the main road but not far. He stared at the curtained window; maybe the room itself was in darkness, but an adjoining one was lit. As he stood wondering what to do, he realized that he could hear the hum of air conditioners. He took a swig of water; his ears closed off as he drank, but when he stopped the hum remained.

It would be a short detour; he could knock and ask, just in case his family had taken shelter there. He turned down the street toward the river.

He'd been expecting an apartment block, but what he found was a small private hospital. There were no inviting, illuminated signs, but if the occupants had been aiming for stealth mode they should have tried harder: none of the windows or balconies were lit up directly, but they were all showing shades of gray. The glass doors at the front exposed a lobby in a similar twilit state. Matt banged on them with what he hoped was the right compromise between inaudible timidity and any hint of aggression.

He received no response, so he tried again more forcefully. In the corner of the lobby, someone moved: a heavily built, uniformed man talking into a radio clipped to his shirt pocket, glancing Matt's way warily without meeting his gaze, as if hoping to pretend he couldn't actually see him.

Matt swung his arms above his head like a castaway hoping to be spotted by a search plane. The security guard grew sheepish and approached the doors.

"We can't take anyone else," he said, shouting to be heard through the glass. "You'll have to try another place."

"I don't want to stay, I'm just looking for my family."

"I don't know about that."

"If I can't come in, can I give you their names?"

The guard grimaced. "There are a couple of thousand people in here, on top of the patients. They're not on the computer."

"Then let me come in and check. I'm here to take them with me; either way I don't want to stay."

The guard shook his head regretfully. "Can't do it, bro. Maybe when the buses come you can check out people as they're boarding."

"What buses?"

"To evacuate the patients to Subiaco."

"You have contact with other hospitals? You still have phones, internet?"

The guard glared at Matt as if he'd been tricked into revealing a secret, but it wasn't the one Matt had been hoping for. "No, but that's the protocol for a fire risk. The buses will come from Subiaco."

Matt didn't know if this was wishful thinking, but if the hospital chain had the resources to keep the lights on, maybe they really could make a vehicle run, if only in the relative cool of night.

"How long until they come?"

The guard turned his palms up.

"Can I wait in the car park?"

"No problem."

Matt withdrew. There were a dozen or so cars arrayed haphazardly on the lot, but behind them another set were parked neatly between the lines. He hadn't taken the time to examine any of them closely, thinking he'd get the quickest answer just by asking, but now he saw that there were at least three that might have been Selena's.

He walked from one to the other. The third one looked less and less familiar the closer he came, but when he reached a vantage where the license plate was visible, it was hers. He froze for a moment, doubting his eyes; if they'd been on foot they might have followed the same signs of life here that he had, but if the car had still been running why hadn't they driven on farther?

He returned to the entrance and banged again. The guard appeared, stern-faced.

"My sister's car is here," Matt explained. "So they must be inside."

"Yeah, that's easy to say."

"I'm trying to take them off your hands!" Matt protested. "Don't you want three less people to evacuate?"

"Just wait for the buses."

Matt said, "I have a boat." He gestured toward the river. "I can take fifty people to Fremantle, right now."

"Do you have paramedics on board?" the guard asked mockingly.

"I thought you had a couple of thousand non-patients. If there's anyone who can walk a hundred meters, I can take them."

The guard stepped back from the door, then spoke at length into his radio. Eventually, he approached Matt again.

"If you're fucking with me . . ." he warned.

Matt couldn't think of anything to say to placate him. After a moment, the guard unlocked the door.

When Matt stepped into the lobby, his skin tingled strangely and he felt his heart racing, as if his body's shock at the abruptness of the change was threatening to overwhelm its relief.

The guard patted him down and searched his backpack. "What's your name?" he asked.

"Matthew Fleming."

He repeated that into his mic, then told Matt, "They're expecting you."

The bulbs in the stairwell were out, leaving only the glow of green emergency lights. When he reached the first floor, he pushed through the exit into the subdued brightness of a ward.

People were sitting in the carpeted corridors, packing the floor as far as he could see. The place stank more strongly of sweat than disinfectant, and the air seemed to vacillate between a welcome chill and the inside of an armpit, as if each stroke of the air conditioners' compressors left them on the verge of being overwhelmed by the sheer wattage of assembled body heat.

There was a narrow path left between the evacuees. Matt wove his way along it gingerly, asking anyone who met his eyes, "Selena, Jim and Alison Fleming?" Most people ignored him, but a few shook their heads or muttered, "Sorry." Some clutched shopping bags stuffed with papers and items of clothing; others seemed to have no possessions but their phones, which they peered at and fidgeted with, but never pocketed, as if they might be reconnected at any moment.

It took him half an hour to search the whole floor; he moved on to the next. The car proved that they were here, somewhere. Unless he was wrong about the license plate. Unless he'd misremembered it, or hallucinated the match.

A guard on the second floor stopped him and discussed his mission on the radio for a couple of minutes before begrudgingly letting him proceed. "There are surgical patients in the rooms, so don't go traipsing filth in there."

"I won't." Matt looked across at the carpet-dwellers, who seemed more despondent than those below. There was a crying toddler squirming in his father's arms, but everyone else seemed crushed into a defeated silence. How long had they been waiting for the mythical buses? Matt's intestines spasmed and he made a detour into the toilets, which had somehow been kept spotless; every bowl and every floor tile gleamed, even as the air reeked with its own unscrubbable record of the traffic.

He spread sanitizer on his hands and scrubbed his face, afraid he might look so haggard that the world he'd come from would seem even less appealing to his family than this disintegrating city. At least he'd kept shaving on the *Mandjet,* even when it began to feel like a vain self-indulgence, but his hair had gone wild and his bottom lip had split open from the desiccating wind and sprouted an elaborate protruding scab as it tried to heal under constant flexion.

Back out in the ward, he trod slowly through the crowd. "Selena, Jim and Alison Fleming?" he repeated.

A nurse caught his eye. "Are you a relative of James Fleming?"

"I'm his son."

"Can you come with me?"

Matt followed her, a few steps behind; the throng parted for her more willingly than for him. She led him to a room; Selena and his mother were inside, seated by an empty bed.

When Selena recognized him she approached and embraced him. His mother stayed seated, not looking up.

"Dad had a heart attack," Selena said quietly. "They tried a few things, but he died about an hour ago."

Unwillingly, Matt started sobbing. Selena clung onto him until he went quiet.

"What happened?" he asked.

"We were leaving the house," Selena replied. "As soon as he stepped out, he got a pain in his chest. He didn't tell anyone until we'd driven for a while, but then Mum saw it on his face and asked him what was wrong, and we turned back to the hospital."

Matt went and sat beside his mother. He tried to put an arm around her, but she pushed him away irritably.

"Every summer, your father made sure the yard was clean," she said. "There were no dead leaves in the gutters, and there was always a firebreak around the house. We have nothing to reproach ourselves for."

"I know," Matt replied. "It's nobody's fault."

His mother glared at him. "Really? *Someone* must have been neglecting their property to allow it to spread like that."

Matt said, "It's still spreading. So we can't stay here."

"Selena's going to drive me to Leo's house."

Matt glanced at Selena; that was thirty kilometers away. "Are you sure he still has power?"

"No," Selena admitted. "And I'm not sure the car

would make it that far; it was already acting strangely when we left."

Matt said, "My friend has a boat down on the river. We're going to take as many people as we can to Fremantle." He decided not to press things any further; there'd be time to talk about the *Mandjet* later.

His mother turned to him angrily. "Who do we know in Fremantle?" she demanded.

"No one," Matt replied. "But we can't stay here, the fire's coming."

He explained his plans to Selena, then stepped out of the room and approached the guard who stood glowering by the stairwell. Once he had permission, he turned to address the evacuees.

"If there's anyone who wants a ride down the river, I can take about fifty people. Just walk east through the park, then wait by the yacht club; I need to bring the boat there from farther upriver." He glanced at his watch. "We should be leaving at one A.M., and we can stop at any jetty along the way. But it's up to you to get to safety from there; I can't offer anything but the boat trip."

A few people stirred tentatively, but most of the looks he got back were dubious.

"Does your boat have aircon?" a woman asked.

"No, it's got a stinking fishing hold with a melting block of ice."

Matt forced himself not to walk back into the room where his father had died; nothing he said to his mother seemed to be helping. He took the stairs down to the lobby.

"Did you find your family?" the guard asked.

"I did, thanks. I'm going to bring the boat now."

The guard grunted noncommittally; Matt probably looked like someone who'd have trouble finding an acquaintance who'd loan him a surfboard. He waited for the guard to unlock the doors, then braced himself and pushed through.

He walked back the way he'd come; the winding route along the riverbank might have been cooler, but it would have been three times as long. Marching toward the flames against the protests of his body felt like a surreal, interminable torture, the kind of thing his mind might invent while he was aching and shivering in a fever dream.

When he reached the rowing club jetty he couldn't see the trawler anywhere, and his knees almost buckled in despair. Why would Thiru have set off downriver already, when the plan had been to wait until dawn?

He gathered up some loose rocks from the ground, then went to the end of the jetty and hung the flag from the edge, anchored in place by the rocks. Then he lay down on the jetty and closed his eyes. If he'd thought things through before he'd left the *Mandjet,* he could have asked Arun to cobble together a portable VHF radio for him, so he could talk to the trawler from land. Maybe Thiru had decided that the fire was coming so close that there was no chance of a rendezvous here. That was perfectly reasonable. He couldn't have expected Matt to find his family so soon.

Matt got to his feet, packed up the flag, and trudged back up to Guildford Road. He knelt down and vomited into someone's barren garden, then he started shaking, too weak to stand again.

"Brother, where you going?"

He looked up and saw Thiru approaching, but it was hard to be sure it was not a hallucination; Matt had never seen him on land before. He didn't have the strength to call out to him; he waited until Thiru arrived before he spoke. "I thought you'd already gone west."

"No. There was a police boat coming up this side, so I thought I'd make myself scarce."

"Good call," Matt declared. Thiru had his passport on the trawler, but a sufficiently officious prick might still have made trouble over the lack of an entry visa.

He sat down beside Matt. "Let me catch my breath."

"Is the boat tied up?"

"Of course. You found your family or not?"

Matt told him everything that had happened at the hospital.

Thiru shook his head sadly. "Sorry about your father." He glanced toward the fire then got to his feet and offered Matt a hand up. "Better not keep the passengers waiting."

. . .

The engine took six tries to start. "From now on, we leave it idling," Matt suggested. Thiru said nothing, but his expression made it clear that this advice was super-fluous.

Matt had feared that no one would take up his offer, but as the trawler approached the yacht club jetty he counted at least forty people waiting for them. At first he couldn't see Selena or his mother, but then he spotted them near the back of the queue.

He jumped off and secured the ropes, then helped Thiru get a ramp into position. The deck of the trawler sat about a meter higher than the jetty, but the river was still and though the ramp creaked and shifted a little, no one lost their footing coming on board.

When the trawler was untied and Matt was back on deck, Selena approached him.

"I tried the car, but it wouldn't even start," she said.

"Okay."

"Where would we go, if we got off in Fremantle?"

Matt shook his head. "I have no idea."

Only about a dozen people took refuge in the hold, all families with young children in obvious distress from the heat. Matt's mother sat on the crowded deck, her eyes to the floor. He took her a water bottle; she accepted it but stared back at him accusingly, as if he were willfully making things hard for her.

Once the trawler was underway, a group of teenagers came forward, asking to be dropped off at a jetty near the middle of the city. Matt joined Thiru at the helm and pointed out the way, then went to help the kids disembark. As they walked away across the dead grass of the picnic grounds, he saw two patches of yellowish light in the distance. Maybe they'd be lucky.

Another, slightly older group got off at the university boat club, heading for a residential college they'd heard was well-equipped to ride out the summer. Then one of the families left to walk among the discreetly illuminated mansions of Dalkeith, sure that the children's grandparents had a safe place for them all.

After that, there were no more requests to stop.

As they passed under Fremantle Bridge, Selena said, "If we go around to the fishing boat harbor, it's just a short walk from there to the hospital. That's worth checking out, isn't it?"

"Yes." The trawler had sailed straight into the mouth of the river, but the harbor she was talking about was on the ocean, and if there'd been signs of life behind it Matt could easily have missed them. He went to the helm and told Thiru the plan.

The harbor was almost empty; Matt could only see two other boats moored. When they came alongside the jetty, three of the passengers jumped off before Matt had even begun tying up the boat, and they disappeared into the night without a word.

The rest, though, seemed reluctant to disembark. Matt guessed that they'd just wanted to travel as far from the fire as possible, but they had no friends or family nearby.

He told Thiru, "I need to find out what's happening here. Maybe half an hour?"

"No problem."

Selena and two of the passengers came with him. They hadn't got far from the water's edge before they saw the hospital ahead, clearly rationing its power but not blacked out entirely.

The four of them approached the entrance together. There were no security guards, and the doors slid open automatically.

But it was all that they could do to squeeze far enough into the lobby for the doors to shut behind them. Beyond the zone that people were keeping clear for the sake of maintaining that seal, the place was packed like a Tokyo subway carriage.

Selena spoke to a woman beside them. "Is there anyone in charge here? Is there help coming?"

The woman frowned slightly; she seemed as bemused as if she'd just been asked when the next royal visit was expected. "The water's still running. The toilets still work. If we keep the doors closed, it doesn't get too hot."

They walked back to the harbor in silence. Matt stayed on the jetty while the two scouts explained what they'd seen to their fellow passengers, and Selena gave her own report to her mother. After a few minutes, people began clambering off the boat and walking away, but he only counted five departures.

Matt got back on deck and addressed everyone who remained: twenty-two strangers—including two families with small children—plus Thiru, Selena and his mother.

"This is our last stop," he said. "If you think you can get to safety from here, if you think there's someone you can reach, who can shelter you, now's the time to go and find them."

No one moved.

Matt rubbed his eyes, unsure what he'd expected. They were not doing this lightly; they knew what was waiting for them here, far better than he did. All the dark houses that the trawler had glided past, all the pitch-black suburbs he'd glimpsed in the distance, would soon be full of corpses. Even in the hospitals and other sanctuaries, the fuel for the generators would run out eventually, or some overburdened part would fail.

He said, "Okay. Then we're heading for Antarctica, and you're welcome to come. We don't have a lot of food on board, and it's going to be a rough ride, but in a couple of days we'll meet up with our friends, and things should be much better then."

13

"Eduardo's calling," Thiru said. "He needs to talk to you."

Matt was surprised; he hadn't been expecting any contact with the flotilla for another half day at least.

Thiru's expression was stony as Matt followed him back to the helm. He gestured at the radio, and Matt took the microphone.

"Eduardo, this is Matt. What's happening? Over."

"Remember the security code for the armaments safe on the rig?" His voice was faint but clear, as if he'd intentionally turned down the power on his transmitter. "Don't say it aloud, just answer yes or no. Over."

"Yes, I remember it. Over."

"Add it after the decimal points on these coordinates, then meet up there." Matt grabbed a pen and wrote down the numbers.

"Got it. Over."

Eduardo said, "Radio silence. Over and out."

Thiru was not happy. "What kind of trouble is this?"

Matt shook his head. "I don't know. But it sounds like he came looking for us, to keep us from walking into something." He glanced out onto the deck. "We'd better not say anything to the passengers until we have some idea what this is about."

He computed the true coordinates, and Thiru adjusted their course accordingly. Within twenty minutes, Matt spotted the *Sereia*, Eduardo's boat, approaching from the south. The sea was as rough as Matt had seen it, so the idea of attempting a face-to-face meeting seemed ill-advised, but when the two vessels were about thirty meters apart his phone beeped: Eduardo was making a mesh call.

Matt was too anxious now for pleasantries. "What's going on?" he demanded.

"We've got four armed men on the *Mandjet*."

"Have they hurt anyone?"

"Not as far as we know. No one's talking to us, but Aaron got off after they boarded and he says they were locking people in their cabins."

"Got off how?"

"He dived into the water and swam to the *Sereia*. When we hauled him out he was bleeding, but it was from banging the hull, not anything they did to him."

Matt was stunned into silence for a moment; he'd never imagined Aaron had it in him.

"So we don't know what they want?"

"No. But if they're not asking for anything, they must have it already: they want the *Mandjet*, and they're just trying to decide what to do with the people."

Matt felt acid rise into his throat. He glanced toward Thiru, who'd only heard half the conversation. Every one of his friends and family had been on the *Mandjet* when they'd left.

"Then we need to convince them to agree to some kind of orderly transfer." Surely they wanted the *Mandjet* empty, once the crew had shown them the ropes. Thiru's trawler couldn't safely take more than a fraction of its original passengers back until the current occupants had been shifted, but across the whole flotilla there ought to be room for everyone.

Eduardo said, "The *Golfinho* has a leak below the waterline. I've tried to repair it three times now, but we might have to abandon it."

Matt couldn't accept this; maybe Eduardo just needed to be clear what was at stake. "I've got twenty-four extra people here!"

"I know, I can see them."

"Then what the fuck do we do?"

"Is Thiru with you?"

"Yes."

"It's mostly his people on the *Mandjet*. He's got to have a say in this."

Matt put the phone down and began haltingly explaining what he'd learned about the situation. Thiru stared back at him with an expression of increasing anger and impatience, then finally picked up the phone himself and started questioning Eduardo directly.

Matt listened in silence. They had to decide if they were willing to give up the *Mandjet*, with all the food and water it provided, and find places for all its passengers on the remaining vessels. But he did not believe that Thiru's trawler would be safe in the Southern Ocean with more than thirty people, and most of the Timorese ships were close to their own limits. If everyone from the *Golfinho* had to be relocated too, it would only be a matter of time before one of the overcrowded boats capsized.

Thiru spoke emphatically: "I can't tell you that until I've seen what's happening for myself." He was quiet for a while, then he said, "You'd better, no, listen to me, then you'd better send someone over here who can run this boat. No he can't, he needs to come too."

After some more discussion, he passed the phone to Matt.

Eduardo said, "Two of my cousins are going to board the trawler, so you and Thiru can join us and go back to the flotilla. Are you okay with that?"

Matt knew he had to be a part of this, and it would be better if he could keep his family as far away as possible. "Yes."

They sorted out the details, then Matt stepped out onto the deck to explain what was happening, wondering if there was any way he could make light of it to the passengers hunched beneath their shade cloths. He'd already used up his quota of "This is your copilot" jokes on the oceanic equivalent of turbulence.

"There's been a small change of plans," he began. "The aquaculture rig I mentioned before seems to have acquired some persistent squatters who are making a nuisance of themselves. Thiru and I are going to try to resolve that, and in the meantime, two excellent sailors from Timor-Leste named Fernando and Francisco will be taking over the navigational duties here. We'll also be bringing more food and water on board, so . . . no complimentary booze, but those of you who've got past the seasickness might enjoy some Timorese cooking."

His audience stared back at him with expressions ranging from bemusement to dismay, but the promise of food seemed to mollify them a little. Selena did not look happy, though, and after a moment she got to her feet and approached him.

"Are you going to tell me what's going on?"

Matt took her into the wheelhouse. "There are a few people on the *Mandjet* we didn't actually invite," he said. "'Squatters' might not be quite the right word for them; maybe I should have said 'gate crashers.'"

"You mean pirates?"

"I don't think we should start flinging labels around."

"But they've got weapons?"

Matt said, "I haven't seen anything myself yet. Thiru and I are going to take a closer look."

Selena looked to Thiru as if he might offer her more details, but he just held up his hands. "Excuse me, I need to prepare for the new crew."

He walked out, and she turned back to Matt. "Are we in danger?"

Matt shook his head vehemently. "Not at all. It's one small group, and they don't even know this boat exists. They're only interested in the *Mandjet*."

"Then give it to them!"

"It's not that simple," he said. "We don't have a lot of extra berths."

Selena understood, but she didn't seem to want to accept what it implied. "You can't bring us out here, and then just . . ."

"Just what? I brought you here, and now I'm going to do my best to make sure that wasn't a mistake."

"We need you with us."

Matt laughed. "Okay. I'll try not to go far."

"It's not a fucking joke!" Selena seemed to be on the verge of tears now.

Matt reached out and embraced her tightly, then said,

"I get to play bouncer with our gate crashers, but you get the hardest job: trying to keep Mum from spinning out of control."

Selena didn't find that funny either. "I'm the one she blames for Dad's heart attack."

Matt grimaced in disbelief. "That's just shock. This is all too much for her. It's too much for everyone." He thought of the dark, sweltering suburbs, and the secrets that now lay rotting in the houses. But they were here in the cool water now, dodging fragments of icebergs; he wasn't going to let anyone rob them of that reprieve.

"Do you think I should talk to her before I go?" he asked. "She seems angry with me too, but I don't know what for."

Selena said, "She blames you for Taraxippus, because you'd never shut up about it. She blames you for bringing the sun so close."

• • •

The crew of the *Sereia* lowered one of their lifeboats into the ocean on ropes, with Fernando on board and some provisions for the Australian refugees. Matt watched the fifteen-meter waves sweep the boat away to the east before Thiru chased after it; getting the trawler's own ropes to Fernando was like trying to hook a prize in some rigged arcade game, but once he had them tied in place, the powered winch made it easy to raise him, and the derrick was long enough to keep the lifeboat from bumping the side of the hull.

Fernando clambered out, grim-faced and unsteady on his feet at first, but he soon recovered his composure. Matt introduced him to Selena, and pointed to his mother who sat scowling on the deck. "Everyone be safe," Fernando promised him, then embraced him like a comrade heading off to war.

Matt helped unload the cargo, then strapped himself into the lifeboat and tried to prepare for the same journey in reverse. Swinging above the heaving deck felt less like anything he'd done on the rigs, and more like some demented franchise ride in a Gold Coast theme park he'd visited as a child. *Pirates of the Antarctic: Fury Road.*

When he hit the ocean he rushed to untie the ropes; with the trawler out of phase with the lifeboat, staying hitched too long could only lead to a tangled mess or a capsizing. Freed, he found himself careering down a valley of slate-green water, so deep it hid everything around him. The wind was deafening, masking the sound of the engines nearby. With no motor of his own, he was just flotsam; if the *Sereia* didn't catch him, he could circle the

Southern Ocean ten times before he washed up on any beach.

The valley everted itself into a mountain, and he gazed down at the *Sereia* struggling toward him. The lifeboat was half-full of water already; it was only the inflated hull that was keeping it buoyant, and only the straps that were keeping him in the boat at all. It had probably only been a couple of minutes since he'd set himself loose, but the *Sereia* seemed to be approaching with an agonizing sluggishness, as if every wave that rolled in was carrying it back just as far as it had managed to come between onslaughts. Matt felt his teeth chattering, though the water wasn't cold. He put his head down between his knees for a few seconds, trying to clear his mind and focus on the task to come. Eduardo wouldn't fuck this up, let alone abandon him. But how smoothly the next part went would be entirely in his own hands.

The *Sereia* came beside him, and Francisco threw the rope down. Matt caught it and held on tight, struggling to maintain his grip as the tension rose and Francisco threw more over the side, then fighting to control the thrashing as a part of it fell slackly into the churning water. But he got it hitched and secured, and then he gestured with outstretched hands back to Francisco, who grinned and obliged him. The lifeboat bumped against the hull and rebounded, sending the rope into the water; Matt was beginning to wonder why the theme park safety rules didn't stretch to a crash helmet. Francisco reeled the rope back in, then tried again.

Once he had three ropes secured, the crew of the *Sereia* winched him up with muscle power and the magic of a block and tackle, continuing the mismatched bumping game between the two boats until he was clear of the hull. When he felt the deck touch the bottom of the lifeboat, he unstrapped himself and rolled out, afraid that if he didn't move quickly his legs would turn to water.

When Francisco saw Matt's face, he seemed to quail a little himself, but his friends gathered around him, clasping his shoulders and shouting things that were probably encouraging. As he climbed into the lifeboat, Matt turned to the nearest crew member and asked if he could help, but the man shook his head and gestured toward the wheelhouse.

Matt didn't want to disturb Eduardo in the middle of all these delicate maneuvers, so he just stepped back and watched as the third crossing got underway. Then he spotted Aaron, looking on from the other side of the deck, and approached him.

"What was Perth like?" Aaron asked.

"Grim. But I got my mother and sister out."

"That's great." A long cut ran down the side of Aaron's

face, half covered by a patchwork of Band-Aids, but it looked like it really needed stitches.

"So everyone was okay when you left the *Mandjet*?" Matt asked. "Rosa, Hélia . . . ?"

Aaron nodded. "They didn't hurt anyone. They pointed the guns at people to get them into their cabins, but then they put bolts on the doors and walked away. They'd actually brought bolts with them, and power tools, like that was the plan all along."

"How the fuck did they even get on board?"

"They said they had a sick kid, so someone waved them through for Rosa to see. It must have been a doll wrapped in rags."

Matt had a lot more questions, but he decided to hold off until Thiru arrived to deliver his own grilling. "Yuki and the others will be fine," he said. "We all agreed a long time ago that if the *Mandjet* was ever hijacked, we wouldn't put up a fight. We'd tell them everything they needed to know about the way it worked, and then walk away."

Aaron said, "So that was when you all had homes to go to?"

Matt floundered. "I just meant—"

Aaron cut him off. "I know. They won't do anything crazy."

Matt felt the *Sereia* speed up; Eduardo was chasing

Thiru in the lifeboat now. He sat down on the deck and put his face in his hands. In the darkness of his skull he saw the empty streets again, and the flash-lit bodies of the girl and her dog. At least his father had lived to the age of sixty-seven, and died with his wife and daughter beside him. Across the city, thousands of people must have succumbed to the heat by now, alone and afraid, with no help or comfort.

When he looked up, Thiru was striding across the deck, straight toward Aaron. Matt listened to the debriefing, contributing no questions of his own.

"Exactly four men, no more?"

"Yes."

"You're sure of that?"

"Yes. I saw them all come on board."

"And the guns? They all had?"

"Yes. Each of them had their own."

"What kind?"

Aaron held his hands apart with his elbows bent: shoulder width plus a bit more. "Semiautomatic; the magazines were about twenty centimeters long. They must have been lying in the bottom of the boat, hidden under other things. But by the time they came up from the docking pen, they all had them raised. I was on the other side of the *Mandjet,* so I'm not sure if they even saw me. I ducked down and watched what they were doing;

I tried to phone Yuki to warn her, but she didn't pick up before they got to her."

"So they came in a small boat that could fit into the dock. Where's the big boat?"

"No one's seen it. It must be hanging back somewhere."

"Anyone join them on the *Mandjet* after that?"

Aaron said, "I don't think so. Someone's always been keeping watch, ever since I raised the alarm."

Matt supposed there'd be women and children on the larger boat, but there might be any number of potential reinforcements as well. Four might have simply been the number they thought they'd need to take the *Mandjet,* not the size of the largest force they could muster without leaving their mothership undefended.

Thiru went to speak with Eduardo.

Matt said, "That was quite a swim you did."

Aaron didn't take this as a compliment. "Do you think I should have stayed?"

"No! Everything you're saying is a thousand times more useful than if you'd been locked up with the others."

"Yeah? What exactly is it useful for?"

Matt didn't reply. In the end, it would be Thiru who'd decide if the hostages would face more danger from an attempt to retake the *Mandjet* than they would from shortages and overcrowded boats if they all rejoined the flotilla. But for his own part, he was yet to imagine a plan with the slightest chance of success; if the hijackers kept even a couple of armed lookouts, anyone approaching would simply be mowed down.

He said, "I thought that by going south, we'd get away from the violence: all the thugs would be fighting it out for a place where they actually wanted to be."

"Looks like they crowded each other out up there," Aaron replied. "So we got the worst of the weather, and the dregs of the criminals."

"Maybe the weakest?" Matt suggested.

"Maybe. But if they've been cheated of what they thought they were entitled to, they might be the angriest as well."

. . .

It was late afternoon when the *Sereia* rejoined the flotilla and the *Mandjet* came into sight. Thiru, Matt and Aaron took turns with the ship's one pair of binoculars, scrawling notes about what little they could observe.

There was always one lookout with a gun standing on the deck above the docking pen, and another on the far side of the ring. They had water with them, and weren't shy about urinating into the ocean without leaving their posts. For more than an hour, no one else could be seen, but then as the sun was setting Matt spotted Yuki being escorted from the control room to the fly hut. He couldn't see her face, but at least her captor was neither pointing his weapon at her nor manhandling her. Fifteen minutes later, they returned to the control room. Matt hoped Arun and Jožka were in there with the fourth hijacker, doing their bit to educate the new owners. He believed Arun would have stayed calm, but he didn't want to think about what might have happened if one of these men had been rough with Jožka in his presence.

Once night fell, there was even less to see; the *Mandjet*'s navigation lights came on, and the weaker illumination on the decks could barely compete with the glare.

Eduardo came and sat with them. "I asked around, and between all the boats we have a few handguns and a couple of rifles," he said.

Matt was taken aback. "You talked about weapons, *over the radio*?"

Eduardo was amused. "No one outside Timor speaks Tetum ... apart from the Australian spies who eavesdropped on our politicians when they were negotiating the maritime boundary."

"Ouch. So do you have any snipers who can pick off four targets in rapid succession in a ten-meter swell?"

"No."

Thiru looked to Matt. "This is your boat. You built it yourself, you know every corner of it."

Matt shrugged. "That's true, but what is there to use against them?" He'd never thought to include remote-controlled trapdoors that could dispose of unwanted intruders one by one.

Aaron said, "They're not watching the cobia. If we came up from inside the ring, they wouldn't be expecting that."

Matt pictured it: the four of them emerging from the water, two on each side of the pond, climbing the ladders and crossing the decks so quietly and with such perfect timing that they could surprise both lookouts from behind, seizing their guns before tossing the hapless men into the ocean. But even if that Bond-movie fantasy came true, what about the other two hijackers?

"Is there scuba gear on any of the boats?" he asked Eduardo.

"No, all the diving gear's surface-supplied."

Aaron was defiant. "If I can make it across without scuba gear . . ."

Matt said, "They didn't have lookouts then."

"So we do it with snorkels. Stay below the surface. You really think the lookouts would spot a tiny plastic tube against these waves?"

"Probably not," Matt conceded. "But even if we made

it there unseen, and no one's watching the cobia pond, once we're out of the water we'd still be easy targets."

Eduardo's son, Murilo, approached the group shyly and whispered something to his father. "I need to read him his story," Eduardo said. He scooped the boy up and carried him away, making a game of rocking him in his arms to keep him level as the deck swayed.

In the silence, Matt could hear the ship groaning from the stress of the waves. If they gave up on the *Mandjet* and lost the *Golfinho,* there would be no room left for a single mistake, or a moment of bad luck. Whatever else went wrong would kill people.

He turned to Thiru. "What do we do?"

Thiru said, "We take turns sleeping, and keep up the watch."

· · ·

When Matt woke, the clouds in the east were turning pink with the dawn. He rolled off his blanket and staggered over to the port side of the deck.

"Anything interesting?" he asked Aaron.

"Both of the lookouts changed shifts," Aaron replied. "After they were relieved, they walked around to the toilet."

That wasn't much of a surprise. Whatever they'd

grown accustomed to on their own boat—and despite their willingness to piss over the side when they were required to remain at their posts—why wouldn't they avail themselves of the most comfortable facilities, whenever possible?

"That's got to be something we can use," Aaron insisted. "Maybe if we wait down in the pond until the shift changes, we can lock one of them in. Power tools and bolts would be too slow and noisy, but maybe someone has superglue."

Matt said, "Lock someone in and they'll just make a noise and attract attention."

"They're still out of the fight, though, aren't they?"

"If the first thing they do is scream 'kill the hostages,' then no, they're not out of the fight."

"Okay." But Aaron wasn't giving up. "Then we go in before they do, and ambush them. Make sure they can't make a noise."

Matt felt sick: this almost sounded like a real plan. An assailant waiting beside the door could certainly surprise someone entering the toilet, though since none of the guns they could obtain would have silencers, the only thing that would work would be a very fast and determined garroting.

And all of it relied on a prior miracle. "Getting up there from the pond would still be too dangerous."

Aaron wasn't happy with this verdict, but he didn't argue. He waited while Matt went to answer his own call of nature, then handed over the binoculars.

Matt settled into position, lying on his belly propped up with his elbows, sweeping the binoculars back and forth until he'd located both of the new lookouts. *When they went off shift, would they be expected somewhere?*

"Were the two of them relieved at different times?" he called out to Aaron.

"Yes. About an hour apart."

"And where did they go, after the toilet?"

"To the mess. Then to their cabins."

"Cabins, plural? They all have one each?"

"Well, these two guys went to different ones. I can't swear that no one else ever uses them."

Matt stopped asking questions and tried to concentrate on the *Mandjet*, but Aaron's scenario kept playing out in his head. If each hijacker silently vanished precisely when their comrades expected them to be lying asleep in a cabin all their own, how long would it take the dwindling group of survivors to realize what was happening? Creeping up unnoticed from the cobia pond was wishful thinking, but there was another way.

He didn't want to be a killer; he didn't even want to risk his own life in the attempt. But if it was a choice between that and Selena and his mother on a lifeboat, Eduardo's family on a lifeboat, Thiru's nieces and nephews drowning as the overcrowded trawler capsized, it would be monstrous to stay silent and pretend that he had no idea how to fix Aaron's flawed plan.

He waited for Thiru to wake and join them. Then he put down the binoculars and told Aaron to repeat what he'd seen.

Thiru was unimpressed.

Matt said, "The thing is, I think we can get into the toilet without anyone seeing us. But we don't go through the cobia pond. We go through the inside of the pontoon."

They both got his meaning at once, but he sketched out the details. There was a service hatch on the underside of every pontoon, and though it wasn't intended to be opened while the thing was immersed, it would just be a matter of someone unscrewing a few bolts, moving the panel away to let the team through, then replacing everything so the water didn't keep sloshing in.

There was also a hatch in the toilet that was meant to grant access to the plumbing if anything went wrong—and when he'd been completing the design, Matt had been claustrophobic enough to ensure that it could be opened from either side. He'd had no intention of ending up trapped among the sewage pipes because the thing had swung shut from the rocking of the *Mand-*

jet.

Thiru said, "It's not going to be simple to work on the pontoon while it's moving." He gestured at the waves. "You can undo a bolt in these conditions?"

Matt had thought about that as he was speaking. "Maybe, maybe not." He wasn't going to make extravagant claims for himself on the basis of welding the *Sophia*'s propeller, when he'd been strapped to a wooden frame that was rigidly locked to the hull. "Maybe no one can. But I know someone who came close."

Eduardo was already up, cooking breakfast for his wife and kids, but it took Matt a while to work up the courage to bring him in on the plan and make a request.

"Will you ask Luís if he'll help us?"

Eduardo thought for a while. Luís had young children, but if he joined the team he would not be coming on board the *Mandjet*; he just had to open the access panel, then close it behind them. "You're sure he can do this?"

Matt said, "I think he has a good chance. There might be someone better, but I wouldn't know who."

"What if I describe the job to everyone, and see who volunteers?"

"Now you want to give away the whole plan over the radio?" Matt joked.

Eduardo said, "I'll take that as a yes. I'll get you an answer within an hour."

Matt went back to the observation post, where Thiru was taking his turn with the binoculars.

"So this guy Luís is joining us?" Aaron asked.

"We'll know in a little while," Matt replied. The more the pieces came together, the sicker he felt. They could plan, and they could argue, and they could joke, but it would all amount to nothing unless it ended with the right four people dead. He could understand if the men had been desperate, but why couldn't they have approached the flotilla and asked for help, like the Sri Lankans? "Maybe we can just gag them," he said.

Thiru was listening. "Don't be crazy. You think the three of us can keep a man with an automatic weapon silent one hundred percent while we shove a sock in his mouth?"

"Have you ever killed someone?" Matt asked him.

"No." Thiru put down the binoculars and turned to him. "And I'd keep it that way if I could. But if these men make one sound, what do their associates do? Slit my mother's throat, my sister's throat? Maybe kill your three friends?"

Matt walked over to the side of the boat and threw up.

Thiru took this as a lesson. "We should fast until it's done. Nothing but water. Vomit when you're trying to swim, and you could drown. Do it when you're trying to take one of these fuckers by surprise, and we could all get killed."

• • •

Eduardo received offers from three volunteers; Luís was one of them. He talked it over with Matt, and they agreed that he'd be the best choice.

"Now we have to get him to the *Sereia* without attracting too much attention," Eduardo fretted. "Maybe we need to fall behind again; the *Sophia* is already lagging."

Matt had no idea what the lookouts on the *Mandjet* would make of the shifting positions of the individual boats in the flotilla. He just hoped there'd already been enough random shuffling from the vagaries of the currents that the *Sereia*'s deliberate trajectory seemed no different.

They fell back beside the *Sophia* and brought Luís on board, the way Matt and Thiru had come. He greeted Matt enthusiastically. "This is a good plan. We can do it."

"Do you need a rehearsal?" Matt asked. "Maybe we could build something here to practice on."

"No, no, no! I had the rehearsal. We need to do this tonight."

The four of them sat with Eduardo, trying to map out each step of the plan. Between the *Sophia* and the *Sereia* they had already assembled enough face masks, snorkels, tools and rope—or at least the rope Luís would need to help hold him to the bottom of the pontoon.

"So what do we use on the hijackers?" Matt wondered, miming the fatal action. "What thickness would work best?"

No one offered suggestions.

"Is there someone we can call who might know?" he asked Eduardo. "João, Martinho . . . ?"

Eduardo was baffled. "Why would they know that?"

"They lived through the occupation, didn't they?"

"Yes. But they were just fishermen. They weren't Fretilin assassins, sneaking through the jungle taking out Indonesian soldiers."

Matt was past caring about making a fool of himself. "Okay, so we've got no experienced killers around except for the four on the *Mandjet*. We'll just have to work it out for ourselves. I'm guessing about five millimeters: that's thick enough not to break under the strain, and thin enough to cut deep into the windpipe. And I'm pretty sure most versions came with wooden hand grips."

Everyone was silent for a while, then Eduardo said, "We have some fishing line like that, and I think I can adapt the grips from a couple of power drills."

• • •

When night fell, Eduardo began moving the *Sereia* into position, then he and Matt worked together to take account of every factor they could think of, so that the team would be transported from their starting point to the *Mandjet* with a minimum of effort.

"I'm impressed that you can still remember the formula for Stokes drift," Matt confessed. "I don't think I've ever used that since my final fluid dynamics exam."

"What's to remember? It's just dimensional analysis: if you screwed up the formula, the units would make no sense."

"Yeah, but one form has factors of two pi in it, and one doesn't. How do you know which is which?"

Eduardo said, "Please stop talking, before I start wondering if I've got that the wrong way around."

He made the final adjustments, then radioed the *Polvo* with the course they'd need to follow in order to pick up Luís—or maybe the whole team, if they missed their target.

Matt left the wheelhouse and joined the others on deck. Eduardo had got everyone else out of sight, sparing the team the distraction of onlookers. In the starlight, the towering waves appeared to be rolling away toward the *Mandjet* with the speed of a fast car, but it was mostly just the pattern of peaks and troughs that was moving, not the water itself, and the final calculations had predicted something more like a slow jog overall—or a fast jog with frequent reversals.

"Don't fight the water," Matt stressed. "When you go backward, it'll only be temporary. Save all your energy for controlling your depth and making sure you can breathe when you need to."

"Okay," Aaron replied. Thiru and Luís just looked impatient. Matt put on his face mask, clipped the snorkel to its side, and bit down on the mouthpiece. The first time he'd been snorkeling he'd been twelve years old, on a family trip to Queensland. He tried to calm himself with the memory of placid turquoise water and bright tropical fish, but the whole reef would be gone now, a skeleton crumbling into white powder.

Luís climbed up onto the side of the boat, facing the deck, and back-flipped into the water. Matt followed, afraid that if he hung back he'd be paralyzed. Submerged, in the dark, his body struck the hull, battering his left shoulder, but as he swam to the surface and blew air out of the snorkel, he looked back and saw that he was already five or six meters away from the *Sereia*. He waited until he'd seen both Thiru and Aaron emerge, then he put his face down and surrendered to the waves.

When he tried to rise again to breathe, he felt himself being dragged down, however forcefully he swam upward. He stopped struggling and waited, counting slowly in his head; nothing could persist, everything was cyclic. *Five. Six. Seven.* Right on cue, the column of water in the snorkel yielded to his cautious attempt at exhalation. He emptied his lungs and refilled them quickly, then the water pulled him down.

The next time he ascended he was better prepared, and he raised his head high enough to catch a glimpse of the lights from the *Mandjet* in the distance, more or less where he'd expected them to be. He was high on a wave, just ahead of the crest—then he was plunged beneath the surface again.

Five minutes. If the pattern persisted, he could keep this up for five minutes. He counted and exhaled, but then took in a mouthful of seawater and spluttered as he went down. He coughed the water out of his airway and tried to swallow it, just to be rid of it, but some pressure gradient between his organs refused to accept the tactic, and the more he pushed the more it felt like a threat to his eardrums, or worse.

He stroked upward, hit the surface, spat out the mouthpiece and the water behind it, then drew in clear air before the churning dragged him down. In the depths, he got the mouthpiece back in without swallowing more water, just in time to take another breath when he rose again.

His confidence was shaken, but he felt his way back into the rhythm. He could still feel salt water sloshing around in his sinuses, but if he sneezed into his faceplate it wouldn't be the end of the world. Better him than Luís.

The more time passed, the stronger the temptation grew to surface fully again to check his progress, but he forced himself to take the danger of being spotted seriously. The lookouts might be bored witless, and expecting a boat if they were expecting anything, but if he stuck his head out of the water into the beam of one of the navigation lights, he would not be inconspicuous.

A minute later he saw the lights anyway, penetrating the water. Eduardo had not mislaid any factors of pi: he'd put the team right on target.

The light intensified, then retreated, then disappeared completely behind the fiberglass of the pontoon. Matt swam down hard then stretched his arms out; he collided with the net and dug his fingers into the holes. The waves wanted to keep playing their dunking game, but he clung on tightly until he'd shifted into a new rhythm, dampened by the inertia of the net.

He clawed his way upward until he reached the point where the net was joined to the pontoon; his motion was now virtually the same as if he'd been lying in his bunk or standing on deck. He was blind, but he could tell that the center lay to his left, from the way the rim of the net sloped down when he was at his highest point. He followed the rim, reaching back with one hand and sliding it along the slightly slimy hull.

His fingers struck one of the crane hooks. He pulled a length of rope out from the coil cinched to his belt, slipped the clamp ring over the hook and spun the barrel to tighten it, then swam back under the pontoon and approached the surface on the outside, rising high enough to breathe just as his lungs were getting serious about punishing him for the delay.

Someone grasped his shoulder. When he turned he could see nothing but a silhouette, but that was enough for him to be sure that it was Luís. For a couple of seconds they were caught in an awkward dance, like two people trying to give way to each other in a corridor, then they crossed over. Matt swam down and found another hook, this one closer to the outer ring of the pontoon, and after securing the rope to it he swam up for a breath then followed the rope back down, past the hook, groping the hull as he went to check for seams and ridges. So far, the plan was working: his rope and Luís's formed an X with its center over the access hatch.

Back outside the ring, he collided with Aaron, and they spent some time checking that they weren't tangling each other's ropes up. Then Aaron continued to complete his arm of a second, taller and skinnier, X. As he left, Luís and Thiru arrived, and the three of them waited, bound to the hull by their ropes, with enough slack to let them rise for air but not so much that they ended up battered.

Aaron joined them, and Luís swam down; he had his sling now, to stabilize him as he worked on the hatch. There were eight bolts: one inset at each corner, and one at the center of each side. Matt knew how tricky it would be to attack them with the pontoon rocking and bouncing in the waves, but the only strategy there was patience: the hatch was not so big that two people could have worked side by side without elbowing each other constantly. Each time Luís came up to catch some air, Matt started counting, and he never got further than ninety before starting again. That was the safety margin, then: if he ever reached a hundred, he'd go down and check that nothing had gone awry.

The twelfth time Luís ascended, he gently slapped Matt on the side of the arm with a plastic bag full of bolts. The plan had been to take out seven completely, and loosen the eighth just enough to pull the panel away from the hull and pivot it around. Luís must have repeated the gesture with everyone, because they all took a final breath then followed the arms of the X

down.

Thiru reached the center first. There was just enough light diffusing through the water for Matt to see that he was grappling with the panel, and then his silhouette wavered and Matt felt a tickling on his neck as a stream of bubbles escaped from the gap and dispersed. A few seconds later, Thiru disappeared into the hull.

Matt waited to be sure he wasn't blocking Aaron, then he unclipped the rope from his belt and moved hand over hand along the *X*, until he found he could poke his head up inside the pontoon. As he clambered over the edge, Thiru turned on a small flashlight—mercifully not pointed straight at him—and the whole fiberglass cave materialized out of the darkness. The layout was familiar from the inspections he'd made during the construction phase, but seeing it now was like falling through an alien portal at the bottom of an Egyptian pyramid and finding himself back in some cobweb-strewn version of his childhood bedroom.

Aaron's head poked up, but then he seemed to be stuck, so Matt crawled over and gave him a hand. The three of them removed their masks and snorkels and sat in the growing puddle beside the hatch, exchanging warily satisfied glances. Then Luís appeared, and took out his mouthpiece. "Good luck," he whispered. Matt nodded, and Aaron gave him a thumbs-up. He put the mouthpiece back in and retreated into the water, then the panel swung back into place. Matt could hear the wrench tapping and scraping against the hull, but he doubted that anyone up on deck could have picked it out against the general creaking of the *Mandjet*.

The loudest noise in the cave was the hissing of the pistons in the wave-power generators at each end. The space in between was essentially a sewage treatment plant, processing excrement and supplying the result to the garden. Matt was surprised that it didn't smell much worse than it did; either the seals were holding up better than he had any right to expect, or he'd simply grown more tolerant. In any case, he wasn't gagging, and his face wasn't streaming with tears.

Thiru lit the way as they crawled along the bottom of the pontoon through the maze of pipes and tanks. The small amount of seawater they'd let in hadn't spread far, but there was a moist, dark residue on the floor that must have long predated their incursion. Above them, there were cabins full of hostages, but it would have taken half an hour with a screaming circular saw to reach them.

Below the toilet, there was a built-in ladder leading down from the hatch. Matt found the sight of it eerie now—as if he'd somehow anticipated what it would be used for when he'd sat tinkering with the CAD file years before—but then, if he'd ever had to come down here to fix a problem, he wouldn't have wanted to go spelunking with a rope, or clambering over the scaffolding of pipes.

Thiru was in front; Matt caught up with him and whispered, "When you get below the hatch, switch off your light and wait for your eyes to adjust. If there's someone up there, you should see the light showing around the rim of the hatch."

"Okay."

When the flashlight went off, Matt froze in the darkness, but no faint circle appeared above them. He heard Thiru turn the handle and raise the hatch, and this time a gray disk materialized, then the flashlight was back on, aimed down toward the foot of the ladder.

Aaron was right behind Matt. They had agreed to cycle through the three roles, but for now Aaron's job was to wait on the ladder so they could pass the first body down to him. Matt nodded to him then ascended, feeling bad about leaving him behind despite the fact that he'd be the farthest from danger. Maybe it was the thought that, if something went wrong, he'd be the last of the three of them to die, alone in this place as the hijackers hunted him down.

Matt followed Thiru up into the room, then Thiru turned off the flashlight and carefully closed the hatch. The darkness was imperfect here—the toilet had a small, opalescent window—but in any case, they both knew the layout, and even in the gloom it was easy to find their way to the door. It was built to open inward, and Thiru took his place by the hinged side, leaving Matt with the earliest unimpeded access to whoever entered. At night, the light was set to come on as soon as the door opened; Matt had agonized over the geometry, but he was sure now that the mirror on the side wall would not betray anything, whichever way their victim happened to glance.

He took the garrote out of the pouch on his belt and tugged cautiously on the handles, reassuring himself that the fishing line remained securely attached. Then he stood with his arms hanging down, keeping his grip loose so he didn't tire the muscles in his forearms. It might be hours yet until the moment came.

The *Mandjet* creaked and hissed as the floor swayed; Matt found himself measuring the waves in his head. *Thirteen meters.* If he lost his nerve now, all three of them would die—and maybe Arun, Yuki and Jožka as well—and even if the hijackers spared everyone else, the ocean would soon claim its share of the survivors. So what had these people expected when they came on board with guns, if not to be killed at the first opportunity? This wasn't a fucking oil tanker that they could seize and then wait for the ransom. They could have asked for food and water, they could have asked for shelter. They'd done this to themselves.

He heard footsteps on the deck and quietened his breathing. He gripped the handles tightly, checked that the loop was wide and clear, then raised it high above his head. None of the hijackers were too tall or too short, and the drop he'd practiced on Eduardo should catch any of them.

Centimeters away from him, Yuki spoke, loudly and irritably. "If you stand outside the door, I'm only going to take longer."

A man chuckled.

"I'm serious. Give me some privacy or we'll be here all night."

"Okay, okay."

She stepped into the room, the light came on, then she closed the door firmly behind her.

As she turned, Matt saw no trace of surprise on her face. She backed away, gesturing to him and Thiru to approach her and join her in a huddle.

"Whatever you're planning," she whispered, "don't risk it. I think we have a deal, and if they stick to it they'll be leaving tomorrow."

Matt stared at her in disbelief, not trusting himself to keep his voice low enough if he put the obvious question into words.

"They think the *Mandjet*'s too much for them to handle," she said. "We blinded them with science, we made it sound like running the LHC. So they're going to take as much stock as they can fit in a trailing net of their own, a big box of maggots, plus one spare water-purifying unit that Arun's set up to run on solar power."

Matt turned to Thiru; he seemed torn between relief and doubt. "You trust them to leave?" he asked.

Yuki said, "Everything they've talked about for the last two days has been about making their own setup work. They really don't want to stay here; they're sure they bit off more than they can chew."

"How did you know we were in here?" Matt asked.

"Arun saw the change in the pontoon's pressure sensor—but don't worry, no one else understood what it meant. He and Jožka are okay, everyone's okay. We just have to hold on one more day."

"Hurry up!" the man yelled from outside.

"One minute!" Yuki shouted back. She went and pulled some toilet paper off the roll, dropped it in the bowl, then flushed. As she washed her hands, she glanced back at the two would-be assassins, waiting for some sign that they wouldn't interfere and try to take things into their own hands.

Thiru nodded silently, then Matt did as well. They moved back into position, out of sight from the deck as she walked out and closed the door behind her.

The light stayed on. Once the sensor had been invoked when the door opened, nothing would change until it reported that the room was empty. Matt was paralyzed for a moment, then he reached up and brushed his thumb over the switch and the room went dark.

"You must be some special kind of lady. I didn't hear a single fart."

"Don't be disgusting," Yuki replied.

The man laughed, and the two of them walked away across the deck.

. . .

Just before dawn, Matt heard footsteps above, and voices speaking in Tamil. Thiru whispered, "They've let some men out of the cabins to help them move the fish."

Matt wasn't sure how the hijackers planned to scoop the cobia up and haul them out of the ring, but he was glad they weren't attempting to make the transfer underwater, by cutting open the net. The stock would replenish itself in time, so long as enough remained to breed.

Aaron said, "How do we know they won't take Yuki and Jožka with them? They're the biologists; they're the ones who can keep it all working."

"Yuki didn't seem to think that was a threat," Matt replied. And if they were prepared to take permanent slaves, they might as well have hung on to the *Mandjet* as well as the experts who knew how to run it. Yuki and Jožka had gambled against that, and all he could do now was trust their instincts until there was a chance to see how things unfolded.

Passing the hours waiting in the dark, listening to grunts and thuds and shouts, Matt could imagine how it must have felt for the people locked in their cabins from the start, with no idea what was happening. But at least there was motion now. The hijackers really were departing—and he did not believe they would harm anyone at the last moment. If they turned their guns on the people at their mercy here, the whole flotilla would remain as witnesses, more inclined to revenge than ever.

Thiru offered occasional commentary gleaned from exchanges between the Sri Lankan men, but late in the morning Matt noticed a shift in their tone that required no translation. People were laughing, subdued at first, but then they were shouting ecstatically, and there were women and children joining in.

Thiru moved toward the ladder, but Matt grabbed his arm. "If they see us appear from nowhere, that could fuck things up, even now."

"All right."

A few minutes later, the hatch opened and daylight

streamed in. Arun called out, "Anyone down here?"

Thiru ascended, and Matt and Aaron followed. Out on the deck, squinting in the sunlight, Matt turned to see the hijackers' boat departing, trailing a circle of bright floats, presumably holding up their own small net full of cobia.

Across the *Mandjet,* people were embracing each other, weeping and yelling. Matt looked around, beaming, infected with their joy, but at the same time he felt as weak as if he'd been beaten all over.

"Are you okay?" Arun asked.

"Me? You're the one who's had a gun in his face for four days."

Arun said, "They were shit people, but they weren't sadists. And Yuki really figured out how to play them."

Aaron and Yuki joined them, then Arun spotted Jožka and called her over. She grinned at Matt and hugged him.

"Welcome back, Captain Matt," she said.

"Don't call me that."

"What was Perth like?"

"I'll tell you later." Matt didn't want to douse the celebratory mood. He could see Thiru embracing Suthan, their faces on each other's shoulders, both of them weeping. "We need to find a way to stop this happening again."

"Metal detectors at the docking pen," Aaron suggested. "And spikes and hot oil dispensers all around the outside of the decks."

Yuki said, "Maybe. But maybe we can also preempt some attempts by making the ad hoc solution official. We *offer* to give away breeding stock, and to teach people how to farm it themselves. The more we make that known, the more stake everyone around us will have in ensuring that the *Mandjet* doesn't end up in the wrong hands."

14

Matt couldn't sleep beneath the midnight sun, so he left the camp and headed west along the shoreline. When he looked out across the water, there was no more hope of glimpsing the horizon behind the assembled ships than if he'd tried the same thing with skyscrapers in Manhattan. Every day the anchorages grew more crowded, and for all he knew the row of vessels stretched right around the continent.

Inland, the ground was thickly covered in moss, and though he'd left the rush of the Mawson River behind, he kept encountering small streams of meltwater that he had to jump or wade across. People had set up camps all along the coast, and he wasn't the only new arrival having trouble adjusting to the perpetual light. Some of the other insomniacs called out to him amiably, some glared warnings, and some looked too shattered to care about a stranger wandering by.

"Are you all right?" a woman asked. She was stooped down in the soil, planting something.

"I'm fine," Matt replied, not sure what he'd done to

look so lost. "Can I ask where you've come from?"

"Zanzibar."

"I'm from Australia. My name's Matt."

"I'm Rayah."

"Pleased to meet you."

She nodded and smiled. Matt approached, but kept a respectful distance, imagining himself stopping at a yet-to-be raised fence around the garden in progress.

"How was your journey?" he asked.

She shook her head sadly. "So hard. But we had one thing to help us: the seaweed. Without it, I don't know if we'd be here."

"Seaweed?"

Rayah explained about the seaweed she and her fellow villagers had grown in nets, long before Taraxippus. When they'd had to leave their homes, at least they'd been able to take that with them.

Matt told her about the *Mandjet*. "Maybe we can trade," he said. "Or exchange ideas." The CRISPR'd flies needed seaweed in their diet, and the *Mandjet*'s own system could always be improved.

"Of course," she replied.

Matt took his leave and headed back the way he'd come. While the sun hung low above the crumbling ice cliffs to the south, above the ocean the moon made a stranger sight. The pattern of maria was still recognizable, but the rabbit he'd known all his life was being slowly pushed aside. In another two years the view from Earth would encompass the whole of the former far side.

As he approached the camp he saw that Jožka was up too, pacing the muddy ground.

"We need sleeping masks," Matt joked.

"I don't want to sleep," she said. "I'm trying to figure something out."

"Yeah?"

"Outside the meltwater zone, the krill numbers are exploding. There are probably more than we can use for food alone, but that won't last forever; as the fresh water spreads, it's going to push the fertile layer down out of the sunlight. So we need to start making biodiesel while we still have the chance."

Matt boggled. "Out of what?"

"We can use krill oil as feedstock," she explained. "You know a lot of these ships don't have enough fuel to make it back north? If Yuki can get the right genes into a bacterium . . ."

Matt left her muttering to herself and entered the tent he was sharing with Selena and his mother. He'd expected to find them both asleep, but his mother was sitting on a folding chair, smoking a cigarette. He'd never seen her do that before in his life, and he was afraid to ask which of their possessions she'd had to trade for it.

"When the summer's over," she said, "what do you think will be left to go back to?"

"Not much," Matt admitted. "We can take a look, but I expect we'll have to stay on the water."

"And then do it all again? Back and forth, forever?"

"I don't know." The further into the future Matt gazed, the worse the prospects seemed. None of the machinery they relied on would last indefinitely. What would the Republic of the South have to trade with the countries that could still manufacture any kind of engine part or computer chip? Jožka's biodiesel? Rayah's seaweed?

"But you want me to be calm?" his mother asked, her eyes narrowed from the fumes. "You want me to accept that?"

Matt knelt down beside her, shaking and sobbing. He didn't know why, he didn't know what had caught up with him. His father's death, the bodies in the houses, the strange grace that had spared him from becoming a killer.

His mother took his head in her hands. "Shh," she said. "It's all right. Everything's all right. I forgive you."

About the Author

GREG EGAN is a computer programmer and the author of many acclaimed science fiction novels. He has won the Hugo Award as well as the John W. Campbell Memorial Award. Egan's short fiction has been published in a variety of places, including *Interzone, Asimov's, Nature,* and *Tor.com.* He lives in Australia.

TOR·COM

**Science fiction. Fantasy. The universe.
And related subjects.**

*

More than just a publisher's website, *Tor.com* is a venue for **original fiction, comics,** and **discussion** of the entire field of SF and fantasy, in all media and from all sources. Visit our site today—and join the conversation yourself.